"*Boo* is an astoundingly original novel and Neil Smith's take on the afterlife is convincing, moving, and often funny as hell. A vision equal parts Murakami and *South Park*."
—Emily Schultz, author of *The Blondes*

"Sad, beautiful, heartbreaking, and impossible to put down."
—Andrew Kaufman, author of *All My Friends Are Superheroes* and *Born Weird*

"A work of singular genius: an adventure story, a mystery, and a profound meditation on childhood, lost innocence, and the power of friendship to save our lives—and afterlives. I believe in Neil Smith's heaven, with all my heart."
—Jessica Grant, author of *Come, Thou Tortoise*

NEIL SMITH
BOO

Neil Smith grew up in the United States and Canada and now lives in Montreal. His first book, the critically acclaimed story collection *Bang Crunch*, was chosen as a book of the year by *The Washington Post* and *The Globe and Mail* and was nominated for the Hugh MacLennan Prize and the Commonwealth Writers' Prize for Best First Book (Canada). He also works as a translator from French to English.

ALSO BY NEIL SMITH

Bang Crunch

BOO

BOO

a novel

NEIL SMITH

VINTAGE CONTEMPORARIES
Vintage Books
A Division of Penguin Random House LLC.
New York

A VINTAGE CONTEMPORARIES ORIGINAL, MAY 2015

The Library of Congress Cataloging-in-Publication Data
Smith, Neil, 1964–
Boo / Neil Smith.
pages cm. — (Vintage contemporaries)
1. Boys—Fiction.   2. Male friendship—Fiction.   3. Murder victims—Fiction.
I. Title.
PR9199.4.S657B77 2015   813'.6—dc23   2014032912

Vintage Books Trade Paperback ISBN: 978-0-8041-7136-6
eBook ISBN: 978-0-8041-7137-3

Book design by Stephanie Moss

www.vintagebooks.com

Printed in the United States of America
10 9 8 7 6 5 4 3 2 1

BOO

DO YOU EVER WONDER, DEAR MOTHER AND FATHER, WHAT KIND of toothpaste angels use in heaven? I will tell you. We use baking soda sprinkled on our toothbrushes. It tastes salty, which comes as no surprise because baking soda is a kind of salt known as sodium bicarbonate.

You never wonder about toothpaste in heaven, do you? After all, you are agnostic. But even believers seldom ponder the nitty-gritty of their afterlife. Thinking of heaven, they imagine simply a feeling of love and a sense of peace. They do not consider whether the pineapple they eat here will be fresh or come from a can. (We actually receive both kinds, though certainly more canned than fresh.)

This book I am writing to you about my afterlife will be your nitty-gritty. One day I hope to discover a way to deliver my story to you.

As you know, I died in front of my locker at Helen Keller Junior High on September 7, 1979, which was exactly one month ago today. Before I died, I had been reciting the 106 elements from the periodic table. My locker number (No. 106) had inspired me, and my goal was to memorize all the elements in chronological order. However, when I reached No. 78, platinum (Pt), Jermaine Tucker interrupted by smacking me on the head. "What the hell you doing, Boo?" he said.

I told you once that my classmates called me Boo on account of my ghostly pale skin and my staticky, whitish-blond hair that stands on end. Some of them considered me an albino, but of course I am not: a true albino has dark red or almost purplish eyes, whereas mine are light blue.

"Boo! How ironic," you may say, "because now our son *is* a ghost." You would be mistaken, of course, because this is not true irony. Irony would be if Jermaine Tucker had said, "Wow, Boo, I truly respect and admire you for memorizing the periodic table!" Respect and admiration are the opposite of the feelings I aroused in Jermaine and, for that matter, in most of my classmates.

Did you realize I was a pariah? If you did not, I am sorry I never made this clear, but I did not want you fretting about something you could in no way control. You already worried enough about the inoperable hole in my heart and had long warned me about straining my heart muscles.

Jermaine walked off to class, and I continued undeterred with my count as scientists Richard Dawkins and Jane Goodall watched me from the photographs I had taped to the back of my locker door. For the first time ever, I reached No. 106, seaborgium (Sg), without stealing a peek at the periodic table hung below the photos of Richard and Jane.

My feat of memorization, however, must have overexcited my heart because I immediately fainted to the floor. I could say I "gave up the ghost," especially in light of my nickname, but I dislike euphemism. I prefer to say the truth simply and plainly. The plain and simple truth: my heart stopped and I died.

How much time passed between my heart's final chug in the school hallway and my eyes opening in the hereafter I cannot say. After all, who knows which time zone heaven is in? But as I glanced around the room where I found myself, I certainly did not see the clichéd image of heaven. No white-robed angels with kind smiles gliding out of a bank of clouds and singing in dulcet tones. Instead, I saw a black girl snoring as she slept in a high-back swivel chair, a book at her feet.

I immediately knew I was dead. My first clue: I saw the girl perfectly even though I was not wearing my eyeglasses. I even saw the title of her book (*Brown Girl, Brownstones*). Indeed, I saw everything around me with great clarity. The girl wore blue jeans and a T-shirt with a decal of a litter of angora kittens. Colorful beads dangled from the ends of her cornrows, and they reminded me of the abacus you gave me when I was five years old.

I lay in a single bed, covered in a sheet and a thin cotton blanket. Other than the swivel chair, the bed was the only furniture in the windowless room. Overhead a ceiling fan spun. Hung on the walls were abstract paintings—squiggles, splotches, and drippings. I sat up in bed. My naked chest seemed whiter than normal, and the bluish arteries marbling my shoulders stood out. I peeked under the blanket and saw I was not wearing pajama bottoms or even underwear. Nudity itself does not bother me, though: to me, a penis is no more embarrassing than an ear or a nose. Still, do not assume that I had found the Helen Keller gym showers, for example, a comfortable place to be. That communal shower room was a breeding ground for the human papillomavirus, which causes plantar warts. And on two occasions there, Kevin Stein decided that it would be sidesplitting to urinate on my leg.

"Excuse me! Hello!" I called out to the girl in the swivel chair, who woke with a start. She stared at me wide-eyed.

"May I assume I am dead?" I asked.

She lurched out of her chair and hurried over, accidentally kicking her novel under the bed. She grabbed my hand and squeezed. I yanked it back because, as you know, I dislike being touched.

"You ain't dead, honey," she said. "You passed, but you're still alive."

"Passed?"

"We say 'passed' here instead of 'died.' Passed, like you did good on a math test." She gave me a smile that exposed a gap between her front teeth wide enough to stick a drinking straw through. When she sat down on the side of the bed, it listed because she was heavy. I once read an article on longevity in the magazine *Science* that claimed that thin people live longer. To offset my holey heart, I tried to prolong my life by keeping a slim physique. Needless to say, my efforts came to naught.

"Let me introduce myself," the girl said. "My name's Thelma Rudd, and I'm originally from Wilmington, North Carolina, where my family runs the Horseshoe Diner." She asked what my name was and where I came from.

"Oliver Dalrymple from Hoffman Estates, Illinois," I told her. "My parents have a barbershop there called Clippers."

"Do you know how you passed, Oliver Dalrymple?"

"I believe I died of a holey heart."

"A holy heart?" She looked puzzled. "We all have *holy* hearts up here."

"No, I mean my heart has an actual *hole* in it."

"Oh, how terrible," she said, and patted my leg.

Thelma went on to explain that she belonged to a group of volunteers known as the "do-gooders." "I always sign up for rebirthing duty here at the Meg Murry Infirmary," she said. "I like welcoming newborns like yourself."

I asked how long a "rebirthing" took.

"It's over in the blink of an eye." Thelma blinked several times. "A do-gooder's always on rebirthing duty at the Meg. We never know when we're gonna get a package."

She patted the mattress, and I eyed the bed, its rumpled

blanket, and its pillow with the indent from my head. The bed did not look mysterious or miraculous in any way. "We just materialize here?" I asked.

Thelma nodded. She gave me a probing look, eyes so deep-set I figured she, too, once wore glasses. "You know, hon, you're the calmest newborn I ever did meet," she said. "You wouldn't believe the hysterics I seen in my nineteen years in Town."

"Nineteen years!?" I said. "But you look *my* age."

"Oh, we're all thirteen here."

This particular hereafter, she clarified, was reserved for Americans who passed at age thirteen. "We call it Town," she said. "Us townies believe there's lots of towns of heaven. One for every age—one for people who pass at sixteen, one for people who pass at twenty-three, one for people who pass at forty-four, and so on and so forth."

"Thirteen," I said, mystified. "You are all thirteen?"

"Townies never age. We stay thirteen all our afterlives. I look exactly the same as when I came here nineteen years ago."

You will find this nonsensical, Mother and Father, but this stagnation in the hereafter saddened me more than the realization of my own death did. I would never grow up, never go to college, and never become a scientist. And, frankly, I had seen enough of thirteen-year-olds back in America—their stupidity, cruelty, and immaturity.

Thelma noticed my sudden distress. "Oh, but we grow wiser the longer we stay here," she said. "Well, at least some of us do."

"Segregating the afterlife by age seems logical," I said to be a good sport. "After all, if the dead were all housed in the same place, Town would be seriously overpopulated."

I then asked, "Will I be here for eternity?"

She shook her head. "No, us townies only get five decades

here. After our time's up, we go to sleep one night and never wake. We vanish in the night. All we leave behind is our PJs."

"Oh my," I said. "Where do we go next?"

"Some say we move to a higher level of heaven, one with better food, sturdier plumbing, and sunnier skies," Thelma replied. "Others wonder if we reincarnate back to America. But the truth is, nobody really knows where we go."

Thelma got up from the bed and opened the door to a walk-in closet. She came out carrying a pair of jeans, T-shirts, boxer shorts, and socks, which she laid on the bed.

"What's your shoe size?"

"Seven," I said.

She went back into the closet to find me some shoes.

"Do you have any penny loafers?" I asked, because they are the shoes you would always buy me, Mother.

"Town has no leather shoes," Thelma called out. "Leather's dead cow and heaven ain't no place for the dead."

While she was in the closet, I slipped the boxer shorts on and then the jeans, which were covered in red, white, and blue patches from the Bicentennial three years ago. "So only Americans come here?" I asked.

"Yep. We don't get no foreigners. Just people who lived in the U. S. of A."

I thought of absurd science-fiction films where the characters on distant planets spoke fluent American English but never Swedish or Swahili.

"What about different religions?" I asked as I selected a tie-dyed T-shirt from the half dozen shirts on the bed.

"Oh, we aren't divided by religion. We get all kinds here. Baptists, Catholics, Mormons, Jews, Jehovah's Witnesses. You name it, honey, we get it."

She came out carrying a tatty pair of sneakers, which had

the letters *L* and *R* inked on the toes. She handed them over. "What religion are you?" she asked.

"Atheist."

She let out a whoop of laughter. "I don't always have much faith in a supreme being myself," she said.

I sat on the bed and put on the sneakers. She sat beside me and picked lint off my T-shirt.

"I ain't religious, but I am a spiritual person," she said. "You spiritual, Oliver?"

"I have never had a spiritual day in my entire life."

She gave me a gap-toothed smile. "Well, your entire American life's over, honey," she said. "But your afterlife's all set to begin. Maybe you'll find yourself some spirituality here."

2	4.00

He

Helium

WHAT DO PEOPLE MEAN BY "SPIRITUALITY" ANYHOW? DO THEY mean they feel instinctively that a higher power guides their life and controls the world around them? Or do they simply mean they feel wonder or awe in the face of beauty? The beauty, say, of a cello concerto in E minor (a favorite of yours, Mother) or of the stratified layers of siltstone, mudstone, and shale making up the Painted Desert (a favorite of yours, Father).

Remember when we witnessed the aurora borealis on a cruise ship to Alaska? We felt awestruck watching gas particles in our atmosphere collide with charged particles from the sun and create arcs of eerie green and pink light that spanned the starry backdrop of night sky. Yet we did not for a moment feel the kind of spirituality that suggested a god (a strapping, curly-headed Zeus, for instance) was crouching behind a cloud with an assortment of colored flashlights to beam across the heavens.

Religious people never think about toilets or toothpaste in heaven, but they often picture the landscape here. They imagine trickling brooks, snow-peaked mountains, thundering waterfalls, and lush forests. They imagine places where they felt awed by natural beauty, where they felt spiritual.

Well, forget the brooks, mountains, waterfalls, and forests. To get a good picture of Town, imagine instead a vast public-housing project. The three-story redbrick dormitories where we live are low-rise tenements. As for the other buildings—schools, libraries, cafeterias, community centers, warehouses—they are plain but solid structures. They are much like the buildings back in Illinois, but with one big difference.

Buildings in Town can "fix themselves."

Over time, a crack in a wall smooths over, crooked steps even out, and loose floorboards stabilize. If, for example, somebody accidentally kicks a soccer ball through a pane of glass, that pane, over a period of weeks, grows back within its frame. Sometimes a bored townie breaks the window in his dorm room on purpose just to watch the glass slowly reappear.

Three weeks after I arrived, I broke a pane of glass on purpose, not out of boredom but rather to conduct an experiment. I did not want to let in the outside noise since I am a light sleeper, so instead I took a hammer to a pane in the shed that sits atop my residence, the Frank and Joe Hardy Dormitory. Early every morning, I head to the roof to watch the sunrise and check the glass growing in the window frame. With a ruler, I measure the day's growth to see whether it is constant. So far, it is not: the glass grows one inch on some days and three on others. Puzzling.

With a jackknife, I cut a line down my left forearm this week. Do not fret, Mother and Father: I am conducting an experiment to time how many days my wound takes to vanish. Apparently, we heal faster in heaven. We are also immune to serious diseases, so the children who died of, say, leukemia need not worry about suffering again. Also, blindness and deafness do not exist in Town, so imagine the amazement and bewilderment of a person like Helen Keller when she awakes in a world she can see and hear.

Does Town fill me with awe? Yes, it often does. Yet in the month I have been here, I have met few people who share my wonder for such banal things as toilets, light switches, and garbage chutes. Flush a toilet here and where does your urine go?

Turn on your desk lamp and where does the electricity come from? Throw an empty pineapple can into a garbage chute and how far down does it fall?

Some townies claim that our garbage falls all the way back to America. They believe that the chutes are a kind of portal back home and that other such tunnels back to America may exist here. I need irrefutable proof before believing in such a phenomenon. To check the depth of the chutes, I recently tied a child's beach pail to the end of a hank of yarn and lowered the pail into a chute. Though I had posted notices about my experiment on all three floors of the Frank and Joe, my dorm mates ignored them and dropped down bags of trash that knocked the pail from its lead and ruined my experiment. No matter. I will try again.

The mode of transportation in Town is ten-speed bicycles. Their paint is often chipped, and their chains sometimes fall off, but they work well enough to go from point A to point B (no riding on the sidewalks, though). The bicycles belong to everybody; in other words, we may not *own* one specific bicycle that catches our fancy. Yesterday I reserved a ten-speed at the bicycle depot and rode it to the Guy Montag Library to spend the afternoon browsing the stacks. I tied the requisite red ribbon to the handlebars to show that the bicycle was in use, but when I came out of the library later, my borrowed ten-speed was gone. One would assume that angels respect rules and do not filch what is not theirs. Sadly, townies have the same foibles as the people of Hoffman Estates.

Another disappointment: our libraries have only books of fiction. How I long for a book on entomology or astronomy! But, no, I must make do with murder mysteries, comic books, literary novels (umpteen copies of *Lord of the Flies*, for example), and young-adult novels about such topics as teen pregnancy and drug addiction. True, Town has no insects, so a book on entomology seems useless, nor does it have teen pregnancy (the only kind of birth here is rebirth) or drug addiction (though there is no marijuana, a boy in my dorm claims he smokes chamomile tea leaves to get "mellow yellow").

Town, in fact, lacks many things Americans take for granted: telephones, televisions, newspapers, high-rises, cars, traffic lights, supermarkets, mailboxes, and much more.

One thing Town has that American towns do not is gigantic concrete walls—four Great Walls called the North Wall, South Wall, East Wall, and West Wall that surround our home and rise an estimated twenty-five stories high. Slabs of concrete the size of dinner plates sometimes fall off the walls and shatter on the ground. The lower sections are covered in murals done by artistic children. Sometimes groups of townies gather at the foot of a wall and scream or sing together in hopes that somebody on the other side will answer back. So far, no reply has ever come.

Town's lucky number is thirteen (on account of our age), and so it is divided into thirteen zones arranged in a patchwork: One, Two, Three, Four, Five, et cetera. (The Frank and Joe, by the way, is in Eleven, near the North Wall.) Some townies imagine Town as a rectangular concrete terrarium and all of us in it as lab mice. They wonder if a terrarium to the south houses thirteen-year-old Mexicans and a terrarium to the north, thirteen-year-old Canadians. They think of our god as a scientist conducting endless experiments in a gargantuan laboratory filled with angels.

How I wish our god were a scientist, like evolutionary biologist Richard Dawkins or primatologist Jane Goodall. (As I told you time and again, you two are the spitting images of Richard and Jane even if Mother insists she looks more like a blond Olive Oyl.)

In my opinion, our god is not a scientist but instead an

eccentric hippie artist. I call him Zig because the name sounds
hip and groovy (hereinafter, Mother and Father, whenever
anyone says "God" to refer to the god running our heaven, I
will change the word to "Zig" in my story to you). I picture
Zig as a skinny man with long hair and a beard, like depictions
of Jesus Christ, though Zig does not wear robes but rather
faded jeans and T-shirts printed with such things as daisies or
the yin-yang symbol. On his feet, he dons flip-flop sandals,
which are popular in Town. In my mind, he smokes marijuana
(not chamomile tea), burns incense, and wears mood rings on
several fingers. Zig must not be a real, honest-to-goodness god
because gods are generally thought to be infallible, whereas
our Zig is always messing up. For instance, the toilets here
constantly get blocked and overflow. As townies say, "Zig don't
know sh*t about plumbing." (Since you are opposed to swear-
ing, Mother and Father, I am softening the blow with an aster-
isk.)

Zig never sends us chemistry sets, astronomy textbooks, pro-
tractors, or periodic tables. Instead, he sends us poster paints,
pastel crayons, chalk, pencils, and markers, all in a full spectrum of colors. We even receive canisters of spray paint (which
explains the graffiti everywhere).

Our father who *art* in heaven (ha-ha).

Zig also sends us instruments like ukuleles, acoustic guitars,
trombones, fiddles, tambourines, and harmonicas. Kids are
musical here, and I would join in if I did not have a tin ear, a
weedy voice, and two left feet. Who am I kidding? I would not
join in even if I had twinkle toes and the baritone voice of an
opera star.

Zig sends us sports equipment as well—footballs, baseball
bats, badminton rackets, basketballs, field hockey sticks. I must
admit I find these items sinister: at Helen Keller, I was regularly

humiliated in gym class. During murderball, for instance, I was always the most savagely murdered, and hence I was never fond of team sports.

In fact, my policy back in America was this: steer clear of others. It is a policy, Zig willing, I will also adopt in Town.

3   **6.94**

Li

Lithium

HEAVEN HAS NO CHURCHES, BUT IT HAS WHAT ARE CALLED houses of good. On the fifth week of my stay in Town, do-gooder Thelma Rudd takes me to the Jonathan Livingston House of Good to attend a punch party. A punch party may sound as violent as murderball but is in fact just an evening cocktail party where the drinks are fruit punch. Thelma is not a girl with a steer-clear policy. She says I, as a newborn, need to get out and meet people to forge friendships—especially since I have no roommate yet.

"But I never had any friends back in Hoffman Estates," I reassure her, "and I never suffered ill effects."

She raises an eyebrow and says, "Oh, baby, don't lie to Thelma."

I think back to my friendless days at Helen Keller. In science class, I had no partner with whom to dissect frogs. Nobody wanted to be paired with me despite the A+ he or she would earn by riding my coattails. Before I adopted steer-clear, I tried at times, especially back in seventh grade, to engage my fellow students in conversation. I first practiced in front of my bedroom mirror because, in the past, things I had said had caused offense or irritation. To my mirror I said, "Hello, Cynthia Orwell. How were cheerleading tryouts today? Did you perform the splits to your liking?" When I said the same thing to the real Cynthia Orwell, she scrunched her nose as though I gave off a foul smell. She said, "Oh, Boo, don't be schizo. Get lost, okay?" I learned I was no good at small talk, perhaps because I do not know how to make talk small.

I try to think of something to say to Thelma as we walk along a sidewalk and bicycles zoom by in the street. Weather is a small topic. I glance into the gray sky with its thin, wispy clouds (cirrus). So far, every day has been warm. I estimate high seventies or low eighties with a drop of five to ten degrees at night. I wish I had a thermometer, but thermometers are another thing Town does without, perhaps because there are no extremes to measure. The weather here is always early summer.

Sadly, there are no birds in the sky. Heaven is without bird life, animal life, or even insect life, except apparently for an occasional specimen that slips in. Maybe Zig thinks Americans tortured other creatures enough back home.

Thelma and I turn down John Clayton Street. The names of streets are written in indelible ink on cardboard wrapped in cellophane. These signs are then taped or nailed to the sides of buildings (as they are in Europe). Buildings, streets, and parks bear the names of characters from novels, and every so often local residents vote to change or update a name. I am about to ask who John Clayton is when Thelma says, "You'd make a fine do-gooder, Oliver."

"Have you been smoking chamomile tea leaves?" I reply. "I'm no people person." I pick up a rock lying next to the sidewalk. "I'm more comfortable with rocks. I'm a rock person. This little friend of mine has iron oxide bands."

Despite the no-bicycles-on-the-sidewalk rule, a boy zips by on a bike with a sparkly banana seat. The handlebar grazes Thelma. "Watch out, lard butt!" he yells.

Thelma grabs my banded friend from my palm and is about to whip it at the cyclist, but she refrains. She closes her eyes and mumbles, "Zig give me strength."

Thelma Rudd also lives in the Frank and Joe Hardy Dormitory, but a floor below me on the second. The do-good council assigned her to be my guidance counselor. She is responsible for checking on me, so she often drops by my room to ask how I am faring. I insist all is fine (actually what I say is "hunky-dory," because you use that odd expression, Mother and Father, and I picture your faces whenever I say it). Thelma often eyes me with a mixture of concern and bewilderment. She must suspect me of hiding something because last time I said "hunky-dory," she said, "Tell Mama the truth."

Some of the older girls—by "older" I mean the thirteen-year-old girls who have been here for twenty years or more—like to refer to themselves as "Mama." They act motherly toward a newborn. They sew patches on the seat of his jeans. They bring him a bran muffin for breakfast to ensure that his bowel movements are regular. They call him "honey," "sweetie," "baby," and "pet."

Ever since I told Thelma that you, Mother, are a fan of jazz standards, she has been singing me bedtime lullabies from the American songbook. I may be past the lullaby age, but in Thelma's eyes, I am still a newborn. Last night she chose "Begin the Beguine."

On Merricat Blackwood Street, Thelma stops in front of an old warehouse where dozens of townies are pushing rattling shopping carts filled with canned goods like green beans, creamed corn, pears, and chickpeas.

Thelma says, "We had a delivery today."

I ask to go in because I have never seen inside a food warehouse. The space is the size of the Helen Keller gymnasium, but instead of bleachers along its periphery, the warehouse has racks of metal shelving that stand high enough that ladders are needed to reach the top. These shelves serve as rebirthing beds for the canned goods, boxes of cereal, rice, pasta, bags of potatoes, carrots, apples, and all the other simple foods we eat here. The food is vegetarian because, as Thelma would say, meat is death, and nothing truly dead can exist in Town.

"Does the food appear in the blink of an eye?" I ask Thelma. "Just like a newborn?"

"Yep, but the food don't come till we remove every single morsel from the last delivery."

We leave the warehouse and continue up the street to the Jonathan Livingston House of Good. It turns out to be a community center with furniture that seems to come from a rummage sale. The miniature fridge and stove in the kitchenette are dented. The wooden chairs around the room are mismatched and chipped. The coffee table is a battered steamer trunk with leatherette handles hanging half off. The plaid couch where Thelma and I take a seat is shabby with quilts laid over spots where the stuffing fluffs through. Hung over the couch is a cuckoo clock with no hands to tell time. Every few minutes, the little shuttered window on the clock swings open and a platform with nothing on it sticks out and then darts back inside.

Most townies at the house of good wear the same purple armband Thelma has around her left biceps. The armband is a symbol of do-goodism. Other than the armband, they dress like everybody else, in jeans and T-shirts.

The boys here, like the boys at the Frank and Joe, have jagged haircuts. There are no barbers in Town, so we cut one another's hair, and consequently some of the boys have bald spots. As barbers yourselves, Father and Mother, you would be appalled. At least hair grows faster in heaven, in the same way wounds and scabs heal more quickly.

Girls' hair is less hacked because girls usually let their hair grow long. The girl who sits down with Thelma and me has long golden hair, the type seen in shampoo ads in America. Thelma introduces us; the girl's name is Esther Haglund. Esther would never be chosen to star in a shampoo ad: she is a dwarf, albeit a tall one (she is about a foot and a half shorter than I am). She has the larger cranium and bulging forehead common among dwarfs.

"Esther's a do-gooder in training," Thelma explains to me. "That's why her armband is light purple."

"Mauve," Esther says. "And I knit it myself." She touches the band around her left biceps.

Thelma points out the pleated skirt Esther is wearing. "Esther makes all her own clothes."

I just stare. I have never been around a dwarf before.

"So how do you like do-goodism so far?" Thelma asks her.

"Well, I'm no complainer, but, Thelma, I swear the residents in my dorm can be pigs sometimes. I make them snacks, organize their school schedules, offer a shoulder to cry on, and even darn their damn socks, and then they leave a Zig-awful mess in our kitchenette and expect me to clean it up. One of them even said to me, 'You do-gooders live for sh*t like this.'"

Thelma shakes her head.

Esther notices my staring. "Do you have a question, Oliver?" she asks.

"Yes, Esther. I was wondering, what type of dwarfism are you afflicted with?"

"*Afflicted* with?" Esther's eyes bulge. "What the hell kind of talk is that?"

"I am having trouble recalling the types of dwarf—"

Thelma cuts in: "He's a newbie, Esther."

"I don't give a fig if he's a newbie or an old boy. That question was plain rude." She turns to me. "We don't say 'dwarf'—we say 'little person.' You got that, kid?"

I nod my head.

Esther reaches for her glass of punch on the side table and then heads off into the crowd of do-gooders in her bowlegged gait.

"I guess I made a friend," I say to Thelma. (This comment, please note, is true irony.)

She pats my leg. "Don't mind her."

"I wonder why Zig doesn't fix dwarfs," I say. "After all, he can fix cancer and blindness."

"Being a little person ain't a disease, Oliver. It don't need no fixing."

I mull this fact over and then ask, "What about children with Down syndrome?"

"Well, some people claim retarded kids come here a little smarter to make their afterlives easier."

"Zig adjusts their IQ up?"

"That's what people say, but who knows if it's really true."

I have a frightening thought: maybe Zig adjusted my IQ *down*. Maybe my IQ was too high back in Hoffman Estates and prevented me from interacting normally with my peers. Mr. Miller, my old English teacher, once said, "Oliver, being over-smart is a handicap." At the time, I thought Mr. Miller was bitter because I had corrected his grammar in class. ("It is easy: 'who' is a subject and 'whom' is an object," I told him as he eyed me with such vexation I feared he would crack his yardstick over my head.)

I do not know my actual intelligence quotient, Mother and Father, since you did not want me tested. You did not want me skipping grades. "You stick out enough as it is," you reasoned, Father. In hindsight, I deem your decision wise because had I never spent time with children my own age, I would be completely out of my element here.

Somebody else catches my eye at the house of good. A boy over by the hors d'oeuvres table is taking quick nibbles of a carrot stick. He is a black boy with an Afro, but he has white splotches on his arms and a few on his face, including a kind of starburst patch on his forehead.

I point out the boy to Thelma.

"That's Reginald Washington," she says. "He's the president of our do-good council."

"He has vitiligo," I say. "It's a disease that destroys the pigmentation in the skin."

"He came to Town like that, but the spots haven't spread none since he got here. He says Zig put a stop to them. One of the reasons he became a do-gooder was to thank Zig."

Reginald Washington claps his hands for attention. He stands at a podium set up near the hors d'oeuvres. "Kindly lend me your ears, my friends."

He gives a talk about do-goodism, the importance of helping others instead of floundering around aimlessly in one's own head. He holds a small bullhorn, which he uses to amplify certain phrases so they sound like the word of Zig. "Do right by others, and they will do right by you!" he thunders as the do-gooders nod their heads—all but Esther, who rolls her eyes.

That do-right tenet is malarkey. For example, I once allowed Oscar Stanley and Larry Schultz to copy from my geometry homework, and did they do right by me? No—the next day, they tripped me as I was walking down the front stairs of Helen Keller, and I sprained my ankle.

I stop listening to Reginald. I prefer to flounder in my own head, thank you very much. I wonder again if my brainpower has fallen a notch in the afterlife. I work myself into such a lather that I feel in mourning for those lost points of IQ. I finally excuse myself and go to the boys' room, where I sit on the toilet and recite the periodic table to make myself feel better.

Be
4   0.01
Borylium

I WILL TELL YOU RIGHT AWAY THAT THE NEXT SCENE IS A DREAM. I dislike stories where a dream is presented, even briefly, as reality. I do not appreciate such trickery and will never knowingly deceive you, Mother and Father.

So here is the dream I have on the night of the punch party: I am lying in the center circle of the empty basketball court at Helen Keller. Along one wall is stretched a banner reading, GO, TROJANS, GO! The me in my dream believes he has been reborn in America because his eyeglasses are on his face and he is once again stark naked. He stands and starts heading toward the gym doors when, in the blink of an eye, the space fills with second-hand supplies—couches, stoves, bicycles, boxes of books, mattresses. So many objects are piled around that he must climb over them in an attempt to reach the gym doors. As he clambers over crates of the same mystery novel (*And Then There Were None*), he hears a pounding coming from the doors. Despite his atheism, he feels that some higher power is knocking. He stubs his toe and twists his ankle as he climbs through the debris, but he finally reaches the exit and swings the doors open. A blinding light greets him. He says to the light, "Are you there, Zig? It is I, Oliver."

Then a voice says, "Are you there, Oliver?" This is where my dream ends. I wake up and realize somebody is knocking on the door to my room.

"It's me. It's Thelma."

"Give me a moment," I call out in a half mumble. After the

punch party, Thelma had said she had an all-night shift in the rebirthing room at the Meg Murry Infirmary. What is she doing back at the Frank and Joe already?

As I slip out of bed, moonlight is streaming through my open drapes. The moon here is full every night. Again, puzzling. I switch on my desk lamp and squint from the sudden brightness. The clock on my desk says a quarter to three.

I shuffle to the door in my oversize pajamas. When I open it, I think for an instant I am still in my Helen Keller dream because standing beside Thelma Rudd in the dimly lit corridor is a member of the Trojans basketball team. He is not in uniform, but I recognize him all the same.

"Zig sent us a late package," Thelma says, but I do not even glance at her because I am looking at the boy.

"Johnny Henzel?" I say.

The boy nods. He stares at me in the same transfixed way I stare at him. He looks thinner than he did in Hoffman Estates. His buzz cut exposes his ears, one of which is bigger than the other. His eyelashes are so dark he seems to be wearing mascara.

"Did you also have a heart defect?" I ask.

"What?" Johnny Henzel says.

"A hole in your heart," I say. The chances of two deaths by the same cause at the same school in the same semester are infinitesimally small, I know, but I am half-asleep.

"Let's step inside," says Thelma, but nobody moves.

Johnny runs his hands over his hair, scratching his scalp and wincing a bit. Finally, he stops scratching and says, "We didn't die from a f*cking heart defect, Boo." His voice is hoarse, shaky. "We got shot by some crazy kid at school."

A scream. Not in the corridor outside my room, but in my mind. A memory of a scream that rang out in the hallway of Helen Keller.

My voice comes out in a whisper: "You must be mistaken."

Johnny Henzel drops his knapsack. He moves toward me and opens his arms. He hugs me to him, his sweaty head resting on my bony shoulder. Even though I dislike being touched, even though I was never hugged by anybody but you two, I do not pull away. I pat between his shoulders gently, the way a mama does, as Johnny Henzel sobs and sobs in my arms.

REMEMBER YOUR FAVORITE STORY ABOUT MY INABILITY TO CRY? The encyclopedia story? The incident took place when I was four and we had just moved to 222 Hill Drive in the Sandpits Apartments so you could take over the local barbershop. You had left me in the den with my plastic dinosaurs while you unpacked dishes in the kitchen. A dreadful racket soon had you scurrying back to the den, where you discovered that the bookshelves on which you had placed a set of encyclopedias earlier had proven too flimsy. Three shelves had given way, scattering volumes A to Z. There I sat among the toppled books, staring placidly into the face of my toy ankylosaur, a dinosaur with an armored body and a bony tail club.

"A whole bookshelf of encyclopedias fell on our little egghead," you said, Mother, in wonder, "and he still didn't crack."

"Our son has the head of an ankylosaur!" you added, Father.

Oh, how I liked when you told that story! I miss you, Mother and Father. Given my holey heart, you must have braced yourselves for my early death, but surely you did not expect my life to be snuffed out by a boy with a gun.

JOHNNY HENZEL DID NOT DIE IMMEDIATELY. AFTER HE WAS SHOT, he was taken to the Schaumburg Medical Center, where he lay in a coma and never awoke. He tells Thelma and me that despite being unconscious, he could sometimes hear what people said to him.

"The doctors even told my folks to talk to me," Johnny says. "They never mentioned the shootings, though. They thought if they did, I wouldn't get better."

It was his ten-year-old sister who told him about his murder. When their parents were out of the room fetching some lunch, she leaned in close to Johnny's head, swathed in its turban of bandages, and whispered, "Gunboy got you!"

"Brenda said my folks refused to say the killer's name out loud. They'd just call him 'the boy with the gun.' She told me not to worry 'cause Gunboy couldn't get me no more. He'd shot himself dead."

"He is dead too?" I say, astounded.

Johnny makes one hand into a pistol and holds it to his own temple. He nods and pulls the trigger.

He and Thelma are sitting Indian-style on the opposite bed. I sit on my own bed, hugging my pillow. I think I am in shock: I did not die from the over-excitement of learning 106 elements by heart.

"Who was Gunboy?" I ask Johnny, whose eyes are still bloodshot from crying.

"I don't know for sure," he replies. "Brenda never mentioned him again. She just kept pleading with me to wake up. 'Open your eyes, Johnny! Please open your eyes!'"

"If Gunboy is a true boy, he must have been a student at our school," I say. "Oh, goodness, he may be thirteen. He may have been reborn here in Town!"

"I doubt it," Thelma says. "Zig may be a dope, but I can't figure he'd ever let in a killer." She turns to Johnny. "You didn't get a look at him?"

"No, not the day of the shooting. I just remember walking down the hall minding my own business. I saw Jermaine Tucker and Cynthia Orwell and Larry Schultz and Oscar Stanley," he says. "I saw you, Boo, standing at your locker. And then nothing."

"If we die in a real horrible way, Zig erases the very last seconds of our deaths," Thelma says. "It's for our own good."

"Gunboy probably shot me in the back of the head," Johnny says. "And got you, too, Boo. You didn't see nothing?"

"I was facing my locker," I say. "But I may remember the sound of a gunshot and even a scream. I am not sure, though. It is all very fuzzy."

"Who at your school would want to shoot you boys?" Thelma asks.

Many a former classmate of mine took pleasure in hassling me and hurting me, but would any of them actually shoot me in the back?

Johnny narrows his eyes. "I think Gunboy was a new kid at school."

"Why do you think that?" I ask.

"I see the b*stard's face. He comes to me in my nightmares."

"Your nightmares?"

"All the nightmares I had at the hospital when I was in my coma. Gunboy haunts me, man. He won't leave me the f*ck alone."

"Maybe you *did* catch a glimpse of him," Thelma says.

"The kid in my dream has an ugly mug, evil eyes, big ears, and messy hair like a punk rocker. I think I might have even seen him around in the months before we got shot."

I try to picture such a boy. But I died on only the fourth day of the school year, so I might not have noticed any new boys. Perhaps he was not in my classes. "It's possible Gunboy killed other thirteen-year-olds," I say. "Other classmates of ours may be here too."

"We can check the rebirthing books at the different infirmaries," Thelma says. "We'll see if Zig sent us any more packages from Hoffman Estates, Illinois." She gets up from the bed and pats Johnny's shoulder. "We'll talk more in the morning, honey. You need to get some sleep."

"Why does he need sleep?" I say. "He was just in a coma for five weeks."

Thelma ignores my comment. She comes over and tries hugging me to her big, soft body, but I have had my fill of hugs tonight, so I move away and climb under the covers. She sings a few bars of "In the Still of the Night" as she tucks in my blanket.

After Thelma leaves, I watch Johnny shuck his clothes and don the striped pajamas Thelma stuffed into his knapsack. As he slides into bed, I wonder if he is afraid to go to sleep in case he falls back into a coma or has a nightmare about Gunboy. But I do not ask. I reach over and turn off the light on my desk. We lie in the dark in silence.

Finally, Johnny says, "I'm glad you're here."

When I do not reply, he goes on: "I don't mean I'm glad you're dead, or passed or whatever the hell they say. I'm just glad I'm not alone. I'm glad a friend's here with me."

A friend. He called me a friend. Odd. We seldom spoke

back in America, but then again, Johnny was shot in the head, so perhaps he does not remember things exactly as they were.

"Good night, Johnny."

"Good night, Boo."

But it is not a good night because not for one minute do I sleep.

YOU KNEW JOHNNY, MOTHER AND FATHER. HE DELIVERED OUR *Tribune.* He seldom stopped by Clippers, though. His hair was shoulder-length, but it was probably shaved off before the surgeons treated his head wound.

I had actually predicted an early death for Johnny back in Hoffman Estates. He was a skitcher. Do you know what skitching is? It is an illegal winter activity whereby a person crouches behind an idling car, grabs its bumper, and then skates down the icy street as the car drives away.

Johnny was a speed demon, as the ribbons he had won as a sprinter on the track team proved. But I saw this perilous activity as a death wish. Furthermore, I saw a paradox because he also served as a school crossing guard. As a skitcher, he flouted the safety rules of the road and risked life and limb; as a crossing guard, he helped younger kids navigate busy roads safely.

I was once witness to his daredevilry, during the winter before our passings. As you know, I always rose early because I could easily survive on six hours of sleep a night. Around six in the morning, I went for my constitutional. Johnny was also up at that hour on account of his paper route, and I would see him around the Sandpits Apartments pulling a rusty wagon filled with copies of the *Tribune.* In winter, a sled replaced the wagon.

One day in January, I came across his sled left in front of a residence on the east end of the complex. I assumed he was inside making a delivery. It was snowing, and little drifts had collected atop the newspapers. I brushed the snow off so the papers would not get soggy.

Sometimes Johnny's dog went along with him on his route. Rover was a drooling basset hound with red, rheumy eyes. I glanced around for Rover, but he was not there. I did see a station wagon idling in the street, though. The owner had just scraped the ice from his windshield and was climbing back into the driver's seat. As he did so, a crouching figure shot out from between two parked cars and grabbed hold of the bumper.

The driver must have glimpsed Johnny in his rearview mirror because he pressed the gas pedal to the floor and his car zoomed down the street. It wove back and forth as though to loosen Johnny from its tail. Johnny finally let go. He tumbled headlong till he collided with a parked car.

I ran up the street to where Johnny lay dazed. His knitted pompom hat was askew. Snowflakes stuck to his eyelashes, snot ran from his nose to his lip, and smudges of newsprint darkened his cheeks.

"It's so gorgeous, Boo," he said, staring at the dawning day.

I looked at the sky, which was a soggy graphite gray like the newspapers lying in his sled.

"Are you hurt?" I asked. "Do you need medical assistance?"

"Lie down. See for yourself how beautiful it is."

"We're on Meadow Lane, Johnny. A car may run us over."

"You only live once." (How wrong he was.)

I glanced around. Nobody was in the vicinity. There were no headlights from approaching cars. The station wagon was long gone.

Who knows why I lay down with Johnny Henzel? I try to avoid nonsense, and yet this act was nonsensical, not to mention risky. Still, I did it, probably because Johnny seemed so adamant.

"Do you see it?" he said to me as the snow wet the seat of my pants.

"What are we seeing, Johnny?"

"Oh, Boo, what we're seeing is peace."

"Peace?"

He lifted a hand in the air and made the V sign with his index and middle fingers.

I looked through his V and saw the delicate outline of a waning crescent moon.

Then we heard the beeping of an automobile. We scrambled up, and Johnny took off toward his sled of newspapers, waving a mitten at me.

In the years he and I lived at Sandpits and attended the same elementary school and junior high, we had few conversations longer than that one in the middle of Meadow Lane last January.

In that fleeting moment in the street, I did feel a certain kinship. I do not know whether to call it friendship. We did share something, but what that something was I cannot say.

8   16.00

O

Oxygen

IN THE MORNING AFTER JOHNNY'S FIRST NIGHT IN MY DORM
room, I pick up his clothes off the floor and hang his jeans in
the wardrobe. I ball up his socks and drop them in one of the
drawers that slide out from under his bed. Yet Johnny sleeps on.

I look around the room. It is tidy and plain. I have not per-
sonalized it in any way other than to hang a drawing of a plant
cell, which I did in pen and ink. Thelma has implored me to
brighten up the place. With Johnny lying in the second bed,
my dorm room now seems more personal (despite his dark, fur-
rowed brow).

It is six thirty. I go to shower. I check my back in the mirror for a gunshot scar, but there is none. Afterward, I go to the
roof of the Frank and Joe to measure the growth of glass in the
shed's window. When I come back, just after seven, Johnny is
still asleep. I write my new roommate a note: "Dear Johnny, I
went to the cafeteria to get us breakfast. Back soon. Hope you
slept well." I sign the note "Oliver," though I realize I will never
be anybody but Boo to him.

I stick plastic containers into a paper bag to fetch us oatmeal. Townies prefer to call it gruel because they claim it is gru-
eling to eat. I exit our dorm, and as I cut across a playing field
to reach the cafeteria, I see a trio of boys laughing and kicking
a soccer ball around. They can laugh and play because nobody
shot them to death, I think. But then I realize I am being unfair:
I do not know how they died, and perhaps their deaths were as
violent as my own.

On the other side of the field, I walk through the front doors of the Sophie Wender School, which houses the local cafeteria. I immediately need to sit on a bench in the lobby because something occurs to me that makes me dizzy and weak. I wonder if Gunboy's bullet is still inside me, perhaps even embedded in my holey heart. My breathing comes in gasps. I remove the plastic containers from my paper bag and stick my nose and mouth into its opening. The bag inflates and deflates with my breathing.

"You okay, Oliver?"

I look up and see Esther Haglund.

"Are you sick?"

I plan to say I am hunky-dory, but I take the bag away from my face and say instead, "I was murdered."

"What?"

"I was murdered," I repeat. "Somebody I do not even know shot me. I assume I died on the spot. The bullet must have hit a vital organ—or maybe it even blew my brains out."

I think of you, Father and Mother. Did you learn the news by telephone or by a police visit at Clippers? I must avoid such thoughts; otherwise I will never recover my breath.

Esther sits beside me on the bench as townies traipse through the lobby of the Sophie. Gangs of thirteen-year-olds jostle, holler, and hoot. They are as happy-go-lucky as my fellow students must have been at Helen Keller in the moments before Gunboy opened fire.

I put the bag back over my face and breathe in more carbon dioxide as Esther watches. She has widely spaced green eyes, which she blinks at me, but she says not a word. She also is terrible at small talk, despite her position as a do-gooder in training.

I put down the paper bag. "You have nice hair," I tell

her—my attempt at small talk. "I should know because my parents are barbers."

She examines the ends of a lock as though checking for splits. Then she pushes her hair back and looks me in the eye. "There's a support group here for murdered kids."

"Support group?"

"Yeah, they call themselves 'gommers.' 'GOM' stands for 'getting over murder.' A silly name if you ask me. Gommers get together and talk about how they passed. Their anger. Their nightmares. That kind of thing."

I must look surprised because she says, "You aren't the only kid here who got murdered, you know. Some gommers consider their death a badge of honor. They lord it over the rest of us. They exaggerate and make their murder more gruesome than it actually was. Hope you don't do that."

I tell her I doubt I will, especially since I did not even witness my own shooting. "I would far prefer a heart defect as a cause of death," I add as I place my plastic containers back in my paper bag. I wonder if a heart defect, common among dwarfs, killed Esther.

Then I stand and say good-bye. I need to fetch breakfast for Johnny and myself.

As I walk away, Esther says, "Wait, Oliver!"

When I turn, she hesitates, but then calls out, "Achondroplasia." It is her form of dwarfism.

"DID ZIG MAKE THE PORRIDGE?" JOHNNY HENZEL ASKS.

"No, the three bears did," I say. This is my attempt at light-hearted humor, but Johnny does not laugh. He shovels his gruel into his mouth and closes his eyes as though the taste is exquisite. He must not have eaten any real food during his coma.

We picnic on the throw rug between our beds. Johnny is still in his pajamas. Considering how famished he is, I forgo my own breakfast and give him the second bowl of oatmeal as well as the cashews, dried apricots, two apples, and two muffins I brought from the cafeteria. While he eats, he leans back against his bed and gives an occasional loud belch because his digestive system is not used to food yet.

I eye his scalp through his short hair. Like me, he has no scar from a bullet wound, which must mean that Zig can double as a plastic surgeon.

"I wonder if my damn picture's up in the school lobby," he says. He reminds me that when Oscar Stanley was hit by a car last year, his school photograph was blown up and put in the glass showcase with a giant get-well-soon card. "Your picture must be there too," he says.

In my most recent school photograph, I wear a T-shirt printed with this Albert Einstein quote: "Education is what remains after you forget what you learned at school." In fact, I would be surprised if Mr. Plumb, our principal, called attention to this quote. I would be surprised if the school paid homage to me at all. I expect my classmates deemed me expendable. "Well, if one of us had to bite the dust, better it be Boo," they probably said. Johnny Henzel's death, however, must have caused plenty of sorrow, since he was a good athlete and a good artist.

I rise from our throw rug, go to the window, and push back the drapes. Because Johnny arrived late at night, he did not get a good glimpse of Town, and so I wave him over. He comes to stand beside me, and as he stares from our third-floor window, he says, "This place looks a little run-down, a little like Armpits."

Armpits, as you know, is the derogatory name some people give to the Sandpits Apartments. It is true that Town is a land of low-rises like Sandpits. "Everything here is very plain and serviceable," I tell Johnny.

"So it's no land of milk and honey."

"No, it's not. In fact, we don't receive either milk or honey here. Zig seems to be a strict vegetarian."

Johnny shakes his head in disbelief. "Thelma told me we're stuck here for fifty f*cking years," he says. "And then we croak all over again."

I tell him some townies even claim that, in the seconds before redeath, we age fifty years all at once.

His eyes go wide.

"I say poppycock till someone shows me proof."

If only I had a movie camera to film fifty-year-olds in their sleep. There are so many experiments to conduct here.

"What if I fall out this window?" he says, looking down at the brittle shrubs and dandelions gone to seed in the Frank and Joe's front lawn.

"You'll probably survive and be carted off to the infirmary."

I recently visited the Meg Murry Infirmary again to collect data on healing times for broken arms and legs. I explain to Johnny that because we mend quickly, some townies act irresponsibly. They ride their bicycles too fast and suffer nasty collisions.

Johnny watches people on bicycles zip by in the street below. He seems almost hypnotized by the procession. I wonder how I will adapt to his presence. I am not used to sharing my space and must already fight the urge to make his bed so it is as tidy as my own. I hope he does not leave his underwear on the floor, clutter his desk with garish knickknacks, or hang color-by-number posters on the walls.

"What happens if we kill somebody, Boo?"

I figure he is worried about getting shot again, so I say, "I doubt there are any handguns here, Johnny."

He turns to me at the window. He is only a foot away. I prefer to keep two feet between me and another person, so I step back.

"I wonder if he's here," he says, looking me straight in the eye. His irises are so dark his eyes look all pupil. I know immediately whom he is referring to.

"Thelma says Zig wouldn't let him in," I say. "But the thought did cross my mind that maybe she is mistaken."

"If Gunboy *is* here, he'll pay the price for turning us into frigging bones in a coffin, man."

"What price is that?" I ask.

Johnny touches a fingertip to his eyelid and then reaches over and tries to touch one of my eyelids, but I jerk away.

"An eye for an eye," he says.

JOHNNY HENZEL'S BODY BACK IN AMERICA IS NOT A SKELETON
yet: it has not been dead long enough to have decomposed fully
in its grave. In a coffin, an embalmed body takes many months
to break down enough to expose bones. The decay depends
on the temperature, the process speeding up in hot summer
months. Johnny's eyes, being softer tissue, would rot first. Of
course, if his body were mummified, decomposition would
stretch over hundreds of years, and if he were buried in Alaska's
frozen tundra, scientists could dig him up in three centuries,
thaw him out, and then flip through our school yearbook and
easily pick out which student lay before them.

Had I died of a holey heart on an Arctic fact-finding mission
and been buried in the ice, I would not mind scientists digging
me up centuries later and putting me in a museum showcase as
an educational exhibit. To me, spending day after day in a science museum is paradise.

At Uncle Seymour's funeral, Mother and Father, you said
you favored cremation, so I suppose you had my body cre-
mated. Did you put my ashes in a ceramic urn and shelf it next
to the *Encyclopedia Americana*? I hope my ashes soothe your
pain. I worry about you. Mother, you are easily distracted and
often forget to look both ways as you cross the highway to Clippers. And, Father, you must not start smoking Camels again.
Remember Uncle Seymour's lung cancer.

I wonder if you would be happier now if you were Christian,
Buddhist, Mormon, or of any other religious persuasion that

puts faith in an afterlife. Would my death be easier on you if you knew that on this Halloween, I am seated in an auditorium at the Sophie and watching a variety show put on by angels?

It is Johnny's birthday today, but alas, birthdays are not celebrated in heaven because we are not getting any older. Here we celebrate only rebirthdays, the date we passed into Town.

Can you guess what costume I am wearing for Halloween? Here is a hint: think of my nickname.

Yes, I am a ghost. I have a white sheet over my head with two large eyeholes cut out by Johnny. His own costume is simply a black domino mask like that worn by bank robbers or Zorro. He said our goal tonight was to disguise ourselves. He also had me clip his hair even shorter. I do not like touching people's skin, but I can touch their hair because hair, which consists mostly of keratin protein, as you know, is dead. Barbering must be intuitive for me, because I did a crackerjack job.

We are far from the only townies in costume tonight. However, Johnny and I are disguised not only for Halloween but also because Johnny fears we might run into Gunboy. On Halloween, townies travel far and wide.

"If he *is* here, he won't want us ratting him out," Johnny said back at the Frank and Joe. "If he sees us, he could attack again. We got to get *him*, before he gets *us*."

So now in the Sophie's auditorium, Johnny twists his head around and scans the crowd for a brown-haired boy with ears that stick out—the boy he still sees in his nightmares in Town. (Since becoming my roommate two and a half weeks ago, he has screamed in his sleep several times. Needless to say, my insomnia is acting up again.)

"There are dozens of brown-haired boys with ears that stick out," I tell him.

We are sitting in aisle seats so we can easily move closer

to Gunboy if Johnny spots him. Our killer will be disguised as well, Johnny says. Maybe as a pirate with an eye patch, Frankenstein's monster with fake bolts in his neck, or the Grim Reaper with a scythe (the reaper I see is carrying a toilet plunger). As you can imagine, zombies are a popular costume since we are the living dead (ha-ha). Zombies wear white face paint with their eyes circled in dusky charcoal makeup. They rub white glue (polyvinyl acetate) into their hair so it stands on end. They wear shabby jeans with tattered legs that descend to mid-calf.

The costumes are homemade because Zig does not deliver the kind of premade Halloween costumes and rubber masks sold in American department stores. Instead, he delivers rolls of fabric and sewing machines so townies can make costumes for their theater productions and Halloween parties.

Halloween is a big holiday here, on a par with New Year's Eve. Fake blood is everywhere tonight. It is made of acrylic paint or ketchup. It drips from head wounds and runs down cheeks. It spots chests. It does not make me queasy, and even if it were real, I would not balk. Remember in sixth grade when my classmates all pricked their fingers and tested their blood type for their ABO and rhesus factor? Some students went white from queasiness. Some felt faint. I did not go white—at least not any whiter. I expected to have a rare blood type, so I was not surprised to discover I was AB+.

I spot Esther Haglund standing in the center aisle, looking for a seat before the Halloween program begins. Her hair is styled elaborately with fancy waves hanging over her big forehead. The blouse she wears is covered in sequins. She squeezes into our row and sits in the empty seat beside me.

"Hello, Esther," I say. "How are you doing this fine evening?"

She stares into the eyeholes in my sheet. "Is that you, Oliver?"

"Yes, I am a ghost. What are you dressed as?"

"A newbie in my dorm gave me this ghastly hairdo," she says. "I'm an actress who plays an angel private eye on TV. I don't remember her name. I passed back in sixty-nine, so I don't know modern TV."

I tell her we watched mostly PBS television at home because my mother and father claimed that the commercial stations rotted the soul. Apparently, you two can be agnostics and still use words like "soul" (I jest).

I introduce Johnny and Esther and ask Johnny if he knows the actress to whom Esther is referring.

"For f*ck sake, Boo, it's that stupid b*tch Farrah Fawcett. Did you live under a rock, man?"

Unlike you, Father and Mother, I am not bothered by cursing. Words like "assh*le," "sh*t," and "c*nt" are just different rearrangements of the same twenty-six letters found in all English words. For me, "c*cksucker" is no more offensive an expression than "weed wacker" or "bumper sticker." I do tell Johnny, however, that if people must swear, they should at least be grammatical. He should say "for f*ck's sake" with an apostrophe and an s.

"People speak appallingly in Town," I add. "They have no adults to serve as grammar role models."

He looks as though he wants to shoot me in the head. "Why you always such a d*ckhead, Boo?"

"Perhaps I possess the d*ckhead gene."

Johnny does not laugh at my joke.

I turn to Esther. "Thelma is one of the performers tonight, but she would not tell me what she will be doing. She wants it to be a surprise."

"She's doing a reenactment," Esther says, rolling her big eyes under her shaggy hairdo. "So get ready for loads of pain and suffering."

"What's a reenactment?" Johnny asks.

"Thelma's a gommer," Esther says. "She's reenacting her murder."

THELMA RUDD IS DRESSED AS A HOLSTEIN. HER COSTUME IS A kind of padded white snowsuit spotted with black felt patches. Where in Town did she get a snowsuit? On her head is a hood with cow ears attached to the sides, one black ear and one white, but the part of the costume that draws the audience's laughter is at groin level: the udder. The four teats look to be made of pink party balloons.

She stands at the edge of the stage, twitching her tail, which is a kind of marionette because it is attached to a string that rises into the rafters.

At the back of the stage, in the semidarkness, stand four trees. I presume they are made of wiring and papier-mâché and their leaves of green construction paper or felt. A single boy steps out from behind each trunk. The four boys stand a few yards behind Thelma with their arms behind their backs. They are big boys—tall and muscular—and look older than thirteen, though of course they are not.

"Moooo! Moooo!" one of them cries out. Then another joins in, then another, till they are all mooing. Louder and louder. *"Moooo! Moooo! Moooo!"*

Thelma smiles sweetly. Nervous giggles erupt from the audience.

Beside me, Esther whispers, "I can't watch this."

The white boys close in on Thelma. They surround her. They carry thin branches, which they use to poke her back, buttocks, and udder.

"It's supper and I'm sure hungry for a burger," says one boy.

"This cow has enough meat on her to feed an army," says another.

"I bet she gives *chocolate* milk," says the third.

"String her up!" says the fourth.

Three of the boys keep prodding Thelma as the fourth boy mimes throwing something skyward. Down from the rafters comes a rope with a noose tied to its end.

One boy says, "She's so fat she'll break the damn branch."

The noose slowly descends to the stage as the lights dim. By the time the noose reaches Thelma, only a spotlight is left, trained on her face.

"For once in my short little life, I wasn't fat enough," Thelma says, slipping the noose around her neck. "The branch held."

Then the lights go out completely. We hear footsteps as the actors move offstage.

Beside me, Esther whispers, "Is it over? Can I open my eyes?"

But it is not over. A voice onstage starts singing. It is Thelma. She is still there.

The song she chose is one of your favorites, Mother and Father. It is a Billie Holiday song about bulging eyes, twisted mouths, and blood on leaves. It is a song about hanging from a poplar tree.

12   24.31

Mg

Magnesium

WHEN ALL THE PERFORMANCES ARE OVER, TOWNIES GATHER IN the Sophie's gymnasium, where black and orange streamers hang from the ceiling and balloons bounce across the floor. In one corner, a group of townies wielding knives is all set to enter the pumpkin-carving contest. Disco music plays on a hi-fi system set up under one of the basketball hoops, and a group of green-faced Frankenstein's monsters do a spastic dance that looks like a conniption fit. Do-gooders—they wear their usual purple armbands over their costumes—pass around trays of a fruit punch called blood. The chunks floating in the drink are not tumors from a witch's heart as claimed but pieces of maraschino cherry.

Some old threadbare sofas and armchairs have been moved into the gymnasium. I sit on a love seat, and Johnny and Esther cram in on either side. I feel their body heat even through the sheet. I can be close to one person briefly without discomfort, but two people simultaneously are hard to bear unless those two people are you, Father and Mother. I wiggle in my seat, and Johnny says, "Oh, I forgot you can't stand being touched."

"Because you got murdered?" Esther asks.

"No," says Johnny. "Even back in America, he hated it. Remember, Boo, in gym when we did wrestling? You were paired with Jermaine Tucker, and when he grabbed you, you went limp like you fainted."

I get up and pull off my ghost sheet. My hair stands straight up from static (or maybe I saw a ghost, ha-ha). The lights are so dim in the gym that in the unlikely event Gunboy is gyrating on the dance floor to "Disco Duck," he will not see us.

I tell Johnny and Esther the story of Uncle Seymour's funeral to explain why I do not like touching others. As you will remember, Mother and Father, his friends and relatives stood around his open casket and talked, mostly about his bakery and how he was famous for cinnamon buns, which were served at the gathering.

Uncle Seymour had always been kind to me. He was an artistic fellow. For my eleventh birthday, he gave me a pretty cake decorated not with eleven candles but with eleven test tubes.

When I saw Uncle Seymour lying in his casket, I realized at once that my dislike of touching applied only to the living. People are ecosystems. The pumping of blood. The dividing of cells. The growing of bones. The killing of cancer cells by soldier cells. It is dizzying all that goes on simultaneously in the human body. To me, two people touching is akin to two galaxies colliding. (Okay, I exaggerate a *touch*, ha-ha.)

Maybe you will say, "But, Oliver, a decomposing body is also an ecosystem, a kind of dying galaxy."

Still, I felt an urge to touch Uncle Seymour. He had such an unusual nose, a bulbous schnozzola with tributaries of purplish capillaries and a field of tiny craters.

I was trailing a fingertip along the cool bridge of Uncle Seymour's nose when Cousin Maureen slapped my hand, called me a ghoul, and shoved me away. As you will recall, I knocked into Aunt Rose and overturned a tray of scones.

"So what you're telling us," Esther says, "is you can touch people if they've kicked the bucket."

"Preferably."

"But we've *all* kicked the bucket," Johnny says.

"Passed is not the same as dead," I say, echoing Thelma. I

scan the crowd for her. I want to commend her for her riveting reenactment.

Johnny rises, grabs hold of my shoulders, and sits me back down on the love seat. Then he plunks down in my lap and throws an arm around my shoulders.

Such proximity is horribly unpleasant.

"Get off me, Johnny."

"Five more seconds."

"Stop it," Esther snaps at Johnny.

"Up yours," he says to Esther. Then Johnny races through his countdown—"five, four, three, two, one"—and stands up again. "You need to get used to it. With practice, you can turn into a normal human being."

Esther gets up from the couch and kicks Johnny in the shin. "Maybe, doofus, we don't all want to be *normal*," she says.

"Look, if he acts like a freak here, kids will sh*t on him just like they did back in America."

Rest assured, Mother and Father, that Johnny is speaking figuratively. Nobody actually ever defecated on me (though, as I said earlier, I *was* urinated on).

Three costumed boys standing nearby must have been watching because one of them, a clown with lipstick and a line of pompoms down his front, yells, "Pile on!" and then they all jump on the love seat. They squirm and wiggle on top of me. Their touch is horrendous, their weight excruciating, and their body odor torture. I almost expect my lungs to deflate, my limbs to snap, and my brain to lapse into a coma.

"Get the f*ck off him!" Johnny yells.

A shoulder blade presses against my face, an elbow strikes me in my side, and a knee jabs me in the groin. I whimper.

Johnny pulls off two boys, a vampire and a scarecrow, and

then yanks the white-faced clown off by the boy's curly red hair (his real hair, not a wig).

I pant as the clown yells at Johnny, "Cool it, assh*le!"

A Halloween song, "Monster Mash," plays on the hi-fi. The singer sings about a graveyard smash as Johnny balls up his fist and punches the clown in his middle pompom. The clown doubles over and falls to his knees. His face distorts, his mouth gapes, and his fingers claw at the floor. He has the wind knocked out of him (medically speaking, his diaphragm has gone into spasms, thus preventing him from inhaling).

Half a dozen do-gooders rush over.

"No fighting!" they yell.

Reginald Washington carries his little bullhorn. "Have you no shame!" he thunders into it. "This is a time of merriment and celebration, and punks like you always ruin it for the rest of us."

THELMA AND ESTHER ACCOMPANY US HOME AFTER JOHNNY IS expelled from the Halloween party. We walk on a street whose name, coincidentally, is Boo Radley Road. It is nine o'clock. The full moon shines and stars twinkle. Both the moon and the stars stay in the exact same place every night. I want to say to Zig, "Change the darn backdrop, will you?" Every decade or two, he apparently does change the arrangement of stars, but we are not due for a new backdrop for several years to come. Forget, however, about trying to locate Draco, Andromeda, Canis Major, Leo, and other earthly constellations: the stars over Town follow different patterns. One of my projects is to map them and create a new system of constellations. Frankly, I am surprised no other townie has thought of doing this.

"Is the sky a trompe l'oeil?" I ask Thelma and Esther as we stroll down a sidewalk lit by streetlamps with round moonlike bulbs sitting atop their stems. Zig turns the lamps on at dusk and turns them off at our curfew of midnight, whereupon the starry sky becomes easier to see. I often scan it at night from atop the Frank and Joe.

"A trump what?" Thelma says.

"An optical illusion," I say, but she and Esther do not understand. "Maybe Zig hangs a backdrop in the sky to reassure us, to make us think we live in an environment like the one we knew in America."

"This place is big on illusion," Thelma says.

We all stop and look into the sky. I think I spot a falling star (in other words, a meteoroid), but in half a second the blip is gone.

Esther says we have the illusion that everything stays the same here, that the buildings around us do not age. Yet the buildings do slowly change over time, she says. Twenty-five years from now, they will have gradually transformed to respect the architectural norms of the day. "We change too," she says. "Townies who arrived here twenty-five years ago are different from newbies who came last month, like you and Johnny."

"In what way?" I ask.

"You know more things," Esther says.

"Like what?" I say.

Thelma answers: "Well, you know about stars like Farrah Fawcett Majors and her bionic man. You know what a light saber is and a lava lamp. You know the words to 'How Deep Is Your Love?' and 'Stayin' Alive.' And you know the names of the brothers and sisters on *The Brady Bunch*."

"I do not know any of these things," I tell Thelma.

"Boo is an exception to the rule," Esther says.

"Johnny probably knows," I say. I look for him. He walks far ahead by himself, with my ghost sheet tied around his neck. For an instant, he reminds me of myself back in America because I was such a loner. I am at ease with solitude, but I do not believe Johnny is. His present solitude, therefore, is much sadder than my former.

"Is your friend okay?" Esther asks me.

I say I do not know. At least, because of his newborn status, he will not be punished for fighting. Newborns are allowed to make blunders for their first six months, whereas the clown who piled onto me will face the do-good council and be grounded in his dorm room for a day or two.

"It's Johnny's American birthday," Thelma says. "Birthdays are hard on newbies 'cause they don't turn fourteen. Besides, first months are always hard. My first months, I was a mess. So let's give poor Johnny time to come around."

"What about you, Esther?" I ask. "Were you a mess when you arrived?"

Esther tosses her big hair out of her eyes. "Oh, I was ever so grateful." Here she clasps her hands against her chest and switches her voice to a higher pitch. "Thank you, dear Zig, for giving me an afterlife." She places her palms together in prayer and adds, "But, my all-powerful, all-knowing deity, does this prepubescent freeze mean I'll never have a real pair of knockers?"

Thelma lets out a whoop of laughter.

As you know, I do not whoop, chuckle, or giggle, but I do crack smiles. Hence, a smile is cracked.

"Hey! Hey!"

"Slow down!"

"Come back here!"

Our merriment is interrupted by shouts in the night. It is Johnny. He runs toward us, in the all-out sprint he was famous for as a member of the Helen Keller track team. He is chasing a boy on a ten-speed. The cyclist zooms past, and I turn and watch him speed away from us and from Johnny. Under the streetlamps, I see the cyclist has brown hair. And big ears.

Johnny runs past us. With his black mask and flapping white cape, he looks like a superhero. He tries to catch up to the bicycle, but his effort is in vain. He comes to a sudden stop under a streetlamp, and the girls and I hurry toward him. Before we reach him, he turns and jogs back to us. He pants because his five-week coma has left him less physically fit.

He grabs a fistful of my T-shirt and bounces on his toes. Behind his Zorro mask, his eyes are wild.

"Holy f*ck, Boo, it was him!"

JOHNNY HENZEL DREW MY PORTRAIT IN SIXTH GRADE WHILE WE
and our classmates at Lakeview Elementary sat under our desks
waiting for the roof to be ripped off the school. A tornado had
been spotted in Cook County that day. The sky outside had
turned sickly green, and winds were howling. We heard the
wind clearly because in weather like this the windows were kept
open so they would not blow in and injure us with flying glass.

As my classmates and I took refuge under our desks on
the dusty wooden floor (what a slapdash job the janitors had
done), Oscar Stanley and Fred Winchester wondered aloud
about deadly tornadoes that had struck the state in the past. I
told them about a twister that had stormed through the county
decades before, torn the roof off a town hall, and sucked away a
town councillor, who was found three days later, at the bottom
of a pond a mile away.

"He was wearing only his underwear," I said. "His other
clothes had been ripped from his body."

Mr. Proman stuck a ruler under my desk and poked me in
my ribs. "Shut your fat trap, Mr. Dalrymple," he said, because
Andrea Dolittle and Patsy Hyde were whimpering from fear.
Poor Andrea Dolittle was known to vomit unexpectedly (for
instance, she upchucked during the testing of our blood types).

Johnny Henzel sat in front of me that year. It was the first
year of elementary school that he and I were in the same class.
We did not talk much to each other. In any case, I paid my
peers little more mind than I paid other bland objects in the

classroom, like a blackboard eraser or a wastepaper basket. The one thing of interest I had noticed about him was the double crown atop his head. A double crown, according to Grandmother, meant two separate spirits inhabited a person's body. Hogwash, of course. (Does Grandmother still believe her dachshund puppy is the reincarnation of Uncle Seymour because of a shared fondness for rum-and-raisin ice cream?)

Under his desk, Johnny held a sketch pad and a pencil. As the winds roared and Andrea, Patsy, and several others girls shrieked and sniveled and Mr. Proman walked the rows of desks growling, "Silence!" Johnny Henzel whispered to me, "Can I draw you?"

I consented. If a tornado did demolish the school and kill me, the sketch might survive and serve as a record of my final moments and a memento for you to cherish, Mother and Father. (Perhaps you have a similar memento today, such as that photograph of me aboard the *Spirit of Alaska*.) It felt odd to pose stock-still for a sketch, however. In fact, no classmate of mine had ever looked at me with such genuine interest as Johnny did that day. As his pencil scraped across the page, I felt the unease—albeit a milder version—that I feel when somebody touches me, so after a while I asked if I might close my eyes.

"I'm done with the eyes," he replied.

I wondered if he would sketch an unflattering caricature. Maybe he would draw me as the ghostlike apparition crossing the bridge in Edvard Munch's *The Scream* (that hysterical fellow and I share a pointy chin). But after forty minutes were up and the principal came on the public address system to announce that the tornado had swept out of the county, Johnny showed me his drawing and it was no caricature. It was, in fact, a good likeness of me, a boy crouching under a desk and waiting patiently for his life either to end or to carry on. I stared at myself, at my wispy hair, my triangular face, and the dark circles under my eyes. "You have talent, Johnny Henzel," I said.

He shrugged and closed his sketch pad. I thought he would offer me the drawing, but he did not. I never saw it again.

Now, two years later, Johnny Henzel again sits on a floor with a sketch pad and pencils, which I picked up at his request from a nearby warehouse using the coupons we townies receive to buy supplies. This time, however, the floor is the roof of the Frank and Joe, and the sky is not tornado-green but rather the usual gray covered in a sheet of clouds. Johnny, the temperamental artist, described it earlier as a sea of fire-extinguisher foam.

As he draws, he talks about secret tunnels to America, the so-called portals that supposedly lead us back home. He heard about them from portal seeker Harry O'Grady, the boy who lives across the hall from us. "You should be out looking for portals, Boo. That's a science experiment worth doing."

"I'm not sure it's a science, Johnny. I think it's more like wishful thinking."

I examine the glass window in the shed atop our building. The glass has completely grown back. The entire gestation period of the window's birth was thirty-one days—about the length of an earthly month. I want to test again to see if I obtain the same result twice, so I take my hammer and strike it against the glass till the window again shatters. Johnny glances up briefly at the noise, and I go into the shed and use a whisk broom and dustpan to sweep up the shards.

When I come out, I remind Johnny of the sketch he did of me during the tornado drill and ask him whatever became of it.

He shrugs.

I tell Johnny that Mr. Plumb, our principal at Helen Keller, should have placed his sketch of me in the school lobby instead of my yearbook picture. I looked more like me in his sketch than I did in my photo. This is a compliment, but Johnny does not reply. His eyes focus on his page. His brow furrows. He licks the tip of his pencil.

My roommate has not showered in days and smells like fried onions. I mention this, and he replies, "Don't stand too close, then."

"Did you not realize," I say, "that the name Oliver is an Irish Gaelic noun meaning 'he who does not stand too close'?"

He ignores my lighthearted banter because he is concentrating on his drawing. This time, of course, he is not drawing me. In a few days, we are to have a meeting with the do-good council from Eleven, and he will bring along what he calls a "wanted-dead-or-alive poster."

Last night, Johnny had another nightmare about our killer. He woke up yelling at around three o'clock, a scream so earsplitting it seemed to pierce every wall, brick, and floorboard at the Frank and Joe. I scrambled out of bed, clicked on the light, and tried shaking him awake, my heart thumping so fast I expected its hole to whistle. Johnny stared up at me, eyes bulging, mouth agape, screams still coming. I had never slapped a person in my life, but I slapped Johnny—so hard I left an imprint of my palm on his face.

He did not want to talk much about his nightmare then, or this morning. I try again. "What happened in your dream, Johnny?" I say nonchalantly as I examine my glass shards, which are all the same size, a half inch in diameter.

Johnny stops drawing. He looks up at the mackerel sky (the holy mackerel sky, ha-ha) and then back down at me. "You really want to know?" he says.

I nod.

"Well, Gunboy was chasing me in Woodfield Mall. He was taking potshots at me but kept missing. He cornered me in that store by the food court that sells beanbag chairs. Then he gave me an ultimatum. He'd let me go if I could explain why I loved life."

"How did you do that?"

"I told him about Rover, what I love about my dog. His bloodshot eyes and fishy breath, his big sighs and meaty paws. How he was proud to be a paper-dog delivering the *Tribune*. And how he read the comics and wanted his own strip like Marmaduke."

"Did Gunboy let you go?" I ask.

"If he'd let me go, you think I'd be screaming my f*cking head off?"

"I suppose not."

"No, Gunboy said my story was crap and he was doing me a favor blasting it out of my brain."

Curious, I ask to see his dead-or-alive poster.

He hands me his sketch pad. "Ring a bell?"

I do not recognize the face from my four days in eighth grade. If the boy had just started at Helen Keller on the Tuesday of that first week, I probably did not notice him. Maybe he was even in seventh grade. Or, more likely, the boy who Johnny sees in his nightmares is not the boy who shot us at all. This Gunboy he sees may be purely a figment of his own imagination.

In Johnny's sketch, Gunboy's face has misaligned features, as though his head were sliced down the middle and glued back together, but not quite evenly. One eye higher than the other. A crooked nose. Big ears out of kilter. Wild, tousled hair.

"He has empty eyes like David Berkowitz."

"Who?" I ask.

"Son of Sam, Boo. You *have* heard of Son of Sam, right?"

"The madman who shot people in New York."

"*Thirteen* people."

You turned off the news, Mother and Father, whenever stories of violence aired. "Our ears are too sensitive," you often said, Mother. So I never learned much about Sam and his son. In any case, news stories were of interest to me only when they revolved around science—fresh observations about the atmosphere of Saturn's moon Titan, for example.

Johnny, however, read about David Berkowitz in the newspaper. "The guy was a lunatic. He said a neighbor's bloodhound was possessed by a god who told him to shoot people. A f*cking nutcase, man. He should have gotten the death penalty."

Johnny stares at his sketch. "Gunboy's like the Grandson of Sam."

"If Gunboy is here," I say, "Zig was sleeping on the job."

Johnny scrambles to his feet. *"F*cking Zig!"* he yells at the clouds. He bounces on his toes and swings his fists at the air. *"Don't you know what the hell you're doing, you son of a b*tch?"*

I try to lighten the mood. "Maybe our Zig was the actual god inside Mr. Berkowitz's bloodhound."

"Huh?"

I adopt the voice of a cartoon dog with a lisp. "Excu*th*e me, *th*on of *Th*am, I'm *Th*ig and I order you to a*thath*inate the people of New York *Th*ity."

I am not normally this playful. Maybe Zig has altered my personality to better suit my surroundings.

Johnny stops shaking his fists at the clouds. He glances at me with a startled look. Then he bursts out laughing.

"What i*th th*o funny?"

He laughs so hard his eyes tear up. He wipes them with his fingers. This is the first time Johnny Henzel has laughed since his passing. I feel prouder than the time I increased the pH of my urine by consuming citrus fruits.

Consequently, a smile is cracked.

15   30.97

P

Phosphorus

ESTHER HAGLUND DECIDES TO CALL OUR KILLER *GUM*BOY. DURING the meeting with the do-good council from Eleven, she draws on her notepad a quick "dead-or-alive" sketch in which Gumboy resembles a smaller, younger version of the clay figurine Gumby. Son of Gumby, I suppose.

She is trying to keep the mood light.

Esther does not sit on the council, but she is here for moral support while Johnny tells the council about our deaths at the hands of Gunboy, and she is also an eyewitness to his recent sighting of a boy who looks like our killer.

The council meets at the Sophie in what seems to be the principal's office. We are seated around a rickety board table with cloudy plastic glasses of water set before us. Johnny, Esther, and I are on one side, and on the other sits the council: president Reginald Washington, vice president Elizabeth "Liz" McDougall, secretary Thelma Rudd, treasurer Arthur "Arty" Hollingshead, and reporter Simon Pivot. On the walls are taped posters from past elections of council members. The poster for the president reads, WASHINGTON = JUSTICE FOR ALL.

By chance, Reginald is talking about justice, but today he does not have his bullhorn to stress certain words. "In my humble opinion, our heaven is founded on justice," he says, "the justice of providing a child who lived only thirteen years with a normal life span." Reginald talks with his hands, like a boy making shadow puppets on a wall. His hands are piebald—brown with white spots. I would like to ask him about his vitiligo—does he believe it to be autoimmune?—but Thelma has instructed me not to bring it up. He is sensitive, she told me. People sometimes call him "the Dalmatian."

"Heaven has never harbored a true murderer," Reginald says. "Personally, I'm not convinced the boy you saw, Mr. Henzel, is your killer. The eyes can play tricks. But if you do discover your Gunboy lives here, we'll need to take measures to ensure he doesn't harm other townies. Our Zig isn't infallible. If he's mistakenly let through somebody who should have been barred entry, well, we may need to act ourselves to seek the justice you and Mr. Dalrymple deserve."

"Do you have jails here?" I ask.

"We have the Gene Forrester," Thelma replies. She is taking the minutes of the meeting on yellow foolscap and now slips her pencil behind her ear. "But few townies get locked up. You got to do something real bad to go to the Gene, like stab a kid or break somebody's leg. If townies get caught stealing bikes, well, they just do community service."

"What kind of service?" I ask.

"Mopping floors, cleaning toilets, chopping potatoes in the cafeteria."

"That ain't enough for Gunboy!" Johnny cries. He holds up his dead-or-alive poster for all to see. "He's pure evil. You can't just have him cleaning the can."

"I understand your anger," vice president Liz McDougall says. Zig prevents dental cavities but, sadly for Liz, does not correct buckteeth. "But our council doesn't usually deal with offenses more serious than fistfights, bullying, and theft."

Treasurer Arty Hollingshead speaks, and as he does, I wonder about the need for a treasurer in a heaven that adopts a coupon- and barter system instead of money. Arty says the council may have to consider a very serious jail sentence if Gunboy is discovered. "Apart from Zig," he says, "there's nobody looking out for us up here, so we must look out for each other and decide what's right and what's wrong."

As the council members talk, Johnny keeps running a hand up and down the basset hound decal on his T-shirt, which I found for him at a clothing warehouse. He strokes the decal in the same way he used to stroke the back of drooling Rover during his morning paper route.

To stop the conversation, Reginald holds up a hand as a traffic cop would. He suggests that Johnny and I go on a bicycle trip to the infirmaries located in the other zones of Town. Even though Johnny spotted the alleged Gunboy in our own zone, that person, Reginald points out, does not necessarily live nearby. "He may reside in Three, or as far away as Six," Reginald says. As council president, Reginald will draw up an official letter allowing us to check infirmary records to see who was reborn on or around the same date I was. Perhaps we will find Gunboy or even another eighth grader who died in Gunboy's attack. With assistance from local councils, we can interview any relevant child. Even if we do not locate an actual student from Helen Keller, we could come across a recent newbie from Illinois who might provide key information on our killer—a name perhaps, or a motive. After all, our killings must have made news headlines.

"To make things easier with the other councils and the infirmaries," Thelma says, "why don't I travel with you boys? As a gommer myself, I might be of service."

"I may as well go too," Esther says. "Because if you find Gumboy, you gommers will need somebody with a level head—so you don't rip off *his* head."

Reginald looks across the table at Johnny and me. He wants to know what we think of the road trip. I am game, not because

I especially want to confront the mysterious Gunboy, but rather because I want to see more of heaven, to verify how things operate in the different zones.

When I answer Reginald, I look at Johnny. "I enjoy travel," I say.

Johnny's forehead is sweaty from nerves, but because I badgered him into showering this morning, at least he does not smell of fried onions. He nods at me. "If we catch Gunboy," he says to the council, "me and Boo should be the ones deciding what punishment that pr*ck gets. Can you promise me that?"

The council members exchange glances.

"We can promise you," Reginald says, "that the punishment will fit the crimes."

ZIG GIVES US NO DIRECT GUIDANCE. HE MAKES NO OFFICIAL announcements. He does not appear in the holy mackerel sky and shout through a bullhorn, *"Do not swipe another townie's bike!"* or *"No food fights in the cafeteria!"* But if we townies delve into the matter of guidance further, we will realize Zig directs us by means of inclusion and omission—in other words, the things he delivers and the things he withholds.

For example, if we stop by a supply warehouse on a delivery day, we will find freshly arrived bars of soap and bottles of shampoo. Zig is telling us to wash our bodies and hair. But we will not find deodorant, mouthwash, or perfume, which he must consider unnecessary. We will find blue jeans and sweatshirts, but no dress pants or tweed jackets. We will find typewriters, but no printing presses or photocopiers.

We will find sports equipment, musical instruments, paperback novels, and vinyl records. The items may look secondhand—some baseball bats are chipped, some books dog-eared, and some albums scratched—but these items tell us something nonetheless. They tell us what Zig deems valuable. In this way, they are our guides.

Johnny, Thelma, Esther, and I are thinking of Zig on the first morning of our road trip when we stop to visit a museum set up in the Guy Montag Library. It is known as Curios (rhymes with "Cheerios"). "The items on display are things we think Zig let slip through by accident," Thelma tells us as we park our bicycles and tie ribbons to their handlebars. (Esther is one of the very few townies to actually *own* a bike. Hers is a smaller model that a bike mechanic redesigned especially for a little person. It is painted pink and even has pink streamers and a pink basket.)

Our group heads up the library stairs to the exhibition space on the top floor. Thelma leads the way. As the oldest townie among us (in heaven years), she likes to chaperone. By the time we reach the third floor, she is winded. "Doggone stairs!" She pants and dabs her forehead with a tissue.

Curios is laid out with a series of small rooms displaying objects in glass showcases, which appear to be aquariums turned upside down. The first object we see on display is a can of corned beef. The product is in an oblong tin. Attached to its side is a simple key used to open the tin. Corned beef is a curious object because Zig sends us only vegetarian food.

"Oh, wow! Far out!" Esther says. "I'm so moved I feel faint. Somebody catch me." (Another example of true irony.)

"Oh, hush up," Thelma says, peering so close to the aquarium that she leaves a shiny nose print on the glass. "I'm feeling homesick. You wouldn't believe how many corned beef sandwiches I ate in my day."

"I *would* believe," Esther says, but Thelma ignores her.

"It's so far from real meat it might as well be vegetarian," Johnny points out. "It tastes like a mix of roadkill and Jell-O."

Thelma reads aloud the typewritten index card taped to the side of the aquarium. The card claims nobody knows where the word "corned" comes from. "This popular luncheon meat," the card says, "contains no corn."

"The word 'corn' once referred to any coarse particles," I say. "In this case, the particles were the coarse salt used to cure the beef."

"How do you know this dumb stuff?" Johnny says, unimpressed, but I know Thelma is thrilled because I can see the gap between her front teeth.

Thelma starts to unpeel the index card from the glass. "I should introduce Oliver to Peter Peter, the curator," she says.

"Peter Peter?" Johnny says.

"His real name's Peter *Peterman*, but people call him Peter Peter."

"He's a square, but Thelma thinks he's a dreamboat," Esther says. "He's the real reason we're here, isn't it, Thelma?"

"Is he is or is he ain't my baby?" Thelma says in a singsong. She tells me to follow her, and she and I head off, leaving Johnny and Esther behind. As we walk through the halls, I glance at other items on display. I see a collection of batteries (D, C, and AA), an avocado-colored rotary telephone, a policeman's nightstick, and a radio, which must pick up only static because there are no radio stations in Town.

We come across the curator next to a small tank of sea monkeys. He is setting up a poster explaining that sea monkeys are in fact brine shrimp, which are closely related to seahorses.

"Hi there, old boy," Thelma says. ("Old boy" is a term of endearment that townies use for boys who have lived here for forty-five years or more.)

Peter Peter does look older, since he has wispy hairs above his lip and more musculature than, say, I do, which is not a difficult feat. I assume, however, that he had lip bristles and muscles on the day he arrived here. Some say old-timers are wiser, given the number of years in heaven they have under their belts.

"I'd like you to meet Oliver Dalrymple," Thelma says to Peter Peter. "He's a newbie."

We nod hello, and I say, "I was unaware Town was home to brine shrimp."

"We do receive occasional nonhuman life," Peter Peter says. "A kitten, a budgie. My personal favorite was Lars, the gerbil that came to heaven in a crate of tennis balls."

"Oh, he was such a sweet little fella," Thelma says. "Remember how he used to stamp his hind legs when he got all excited?"

"Yes, that was a kind of mating dance, except the poor boy had no ladylove."

Peter Peter stares at Thelma. "What a tragedy," she says.

They are possibly flirting, but I am no expert on such matters. I interrupt them with the etymology of "corned beef."

"Of course," Peter Peter says, bouncing his palm off his forehead. "The word 'corn' meant any kind of crop or grain, not only the maize of American Indians. So it makes sense the word refers to anything grainy—like salt."

"I am almost certain about the etymology," I tell him. "How unfortunate that Zig sends us no encyclopedias or dictionaries to verify such things. Unless reference books are among the curious objects in your collection."

Peter Peter shakes his head. "No dictionaries or encyclopedias. At least not yet. But new unusual objects appear all the time, so perhaps a full-edition Webster's dictionary will slip through one day. I can only hope."

Thelma tells Peter Peter that I have a keen interest in science. "Maybe you could use an assistant," she suggests.

"Science?" Peter Peter says. "Well, do I have a treat for you!" He asks Thelma and me to wait for him while he goes to his office on the other side of the hall to fetch something. After he trots off, we notice that the visitors who were giggling around a nearby showcase have dispersed, and the object within is now revealed.

Thelma edges toward the showcase. "Is that what I think it is?" she says.

The object is a square plastic envelope the size of a saltine cracker.

"A condom," I tell her. "A sheath placed on the penis during intercourse as a method of birth control to prevent sperm—"

"Oliver," Thelma interrupts. "You don't need to give me no eddy-mology about that thing, okay."

"I don't know the etymology of 'condom,' only its purpose."

Peter Peter returns from his office wearing cotton gloves. He lays a magazine atop the case holding the condom display.

My heart flutters and hiccups—not literally, excuse the artistic flourish, Mother and Father. I am excited because what the curator laid before me is the magazine *Science*. Glory be, it is a recent issue, from October 1979.

"May I touch it?"

Peter Peter removes his cotton gloves and passes them to me. "To keep oil from the fingers off the paper," he says. My hands tremble slightly as I slip on the gloves. I wonder if the two of you latched on to a way to forward my favorite magazine to me here. An absurd thought, I know.

"When did it arrive?" Thelma asks.

"Just last week from Four," says Peter Peter.

"Are there other issues?" I ask as I examine the magazine, whose cover girl is the beautiful ugly mug of a brown bat. The lead article talks about echolocation.

"Not of *Science*, but other magazines sometimes come in," Peter Peter says. "I have a *Life* from 1956, a few *National Geographic*s, even a movie magazine from the thirties with the Scarecrow, Tin Man, and Lion on the cover."

The librarian at Guy Montag had told me the only magazines usually delivered to Town are comic books, so such finds are indeed curious.

"I wonder if Zig is telling us something by letting these things through," Thelma says.

"Possibly," Peter Peter says. "Or they may simply be an oversight on his part."

I leaf through the pages. "Look, an article on cryogenics," I say.

"Cyro what?" Thelma asks.

"Cryogenics. You know, the popsiclization of death!" (Ha-ha.)

"Oh, Oliver, you look like a curious object yourself," Thelma says.

I continue turning the pages, but my giddiness is cut short by Esther, who hurries toward us. Her face is grim. "You better come quick," she says.

"Johnny?" Thelma asks, and Esther nods. We all follow her back through the exhibition halls, past showcases containing prescription eyeglasses, a bottle of red wine (CHÂTEAU BEL-AIR, reads the poster), and a lunar globe. I am so worried that Johnny may have gotten into a fistfight again that I do not stop to examine the globe.

I see my roommate in front of a showcase in one corner of the room. Nothing looks out of the ordinary, at least not till we gather around him and I see his eyes. They are red and puffy as though he is having an allergy attack. His breath is also wheezy.

"What's wrong, Johnny?" I ask.

Esther says, "Look in the case."

The curious object, lying in its showcase on a white cushion, is a small revolver. It looks like a toy gun; if it were not deadly, it would even look cute. As you will recall, Mother and Father, Uncle Seymour bought one like this to protect himself after his bakery was held up.

"Goodness," Thelma mutters, placing a hand on Johnny's shoulder. "Come away from there," she says, but Johnny brushes her hand off.

"When did this gun arrive?" I ask Peter Peter.

"A week ago, from Six. It can't fire, though. It has no bullets."

"Johnny, this can't be the one," I say.

"How do you know?" His voice is as hoarse as on his first days in Town. "It looks the same, Boo. I swear to Zig it does. Just like the gun I see in my nightmares."

"Guns all look the same," Esther says. "They're all horrid. Let's split, Johnny."

She tries to slip her hand in his to pull him away, but he barks, "No!"

We leave Johnny alone. At Thelma's suggestion, we go over to the doorway to the exhibition hall to wait for him, and then Thelma tells Peter Peter about Gunboy and our mission. We are interrupted by some visitors entering the hall, whom Peter Peter asks to avoid the display in the left-hand corner because "that chap over there is repairing the showcase and needs space to work."

As we wait, Peter Peter asks if I would be interested in a job at Curios. "We could indeed use some young blood around here," he says.

Despite my eagerness, I ask if we could speak of his job offer another time. "I need to watch over my friend right now," I say. I take off the white gloves and hand them back to him.

"Certainly," Peter Peter says. He tells Thelma to drop by again soon for a lunch date and then bids us all adieu with handshakes before he heads back to work on his sea monkey exhibit.

From the doorway, the girls and I continue to watch Johnny. We see him only from the back. He does not move an inch. He does not make a sound.

"You'd think he was praying at a church altar," Esther says. "Like I used to do when I was Mormon in Utah, back when I gave a damn about Joseph Smith."

"Who?" I ask, and she explains that Joseph Smith was the founder of Mormonism. In his backyard, the man dug up golden tablets that contained a god's invisible writings that only Mr. Smith could read. "A crock of sh*t, I'm sure," she says. "But come to think of it, no more far-fetched than this place we ended up in."

As I listen to Esther, I keep an eye on Johnny, on the double crown on the back of his head. When a visitor draws too close to my roommate, I call out, "Give him space to work."

Eventually Johnny turns and walks over to us. His eyes are no longer red. His face looks curiously serene.

"You ready, sweetie?" Thelma asks.

"Yeah, I'm ready," Johnny says. "I'm not scared no more. I'm ready to catch that b*stard."

17	35.45
Cl	
Chlorine	

"SHOW SOME BACKBONE," JOHNNY SAYS. "GUNBOY DIDN'T STEAL your bike, Boo. He stole your *life*."

Later in the day, as we finish our picnic lunch in Jerry Renault Park in Ten, Johnny decides I need boxing lessons to prepare for our battle with Gunboy—who, Johnny supposes, has rounded up a posse of goons we will need to defeat. My roommate and I have taken off our T-shirts. I look like the ninety-pound weakling I am, and Johnny, given his fluid diet in the hospital, is no Atlas either. He stands before me, jaw clenched, staring me meanly in the eye. "Look fierce," he says, and I furrow my brow.

"Boo, you look as fierce as an albino bunny," Esther says. She is eating her cucumber sandwich on a patch of grass infested with weeds, which grow everywhere in Town. Dandelions must be heaven's official flower. Also, the grass is usually really long here because we have no mowers.

Johnny raises his fists to spar, and I think of the expression "put up your dukes" and wonder again about etymology: how did a title of British nobility transform into a fist?

Johnny punches me in the shoulder, and I back away. He follows and punches me again. I look around for Thelma, who should return soon from the nearby cafeteria, where she went to fetch extra fruit for the road. "Thelma wouldn't want us fighting," I say.

"Forget your mama," Johnny replies, "and hit me back."

"But I have no reason to hit you, Johnny."

"I'm not Johnny, damn it," he cries. "I'm Gunboy and I want to snuff you out, you jockstrap."

I raise my fists to humor him.

He bops around and calls me names like "d*ckhead" and "assw*pe." I find the whole exercise pointless. I am about to respond, "I'm rubber, you're glue," to show how childish he is being, but then he cuffs me in the jaw—lightly, but still it hurts. I reason that the only way to end the silliness is to wallop him.

I ball up a fist and swing it at his jaw. *Baf!* The blow hurts my hand. Johnny staggers back. He bends over, hands on his thighs, wincing in pain. "Sh*t," he mutters, and then spits on the ground.

I see a red blob in the grass. "Is that blood?"

"I bit my f*cking tongue."

"Serves you right, Rocky," Esther says.

Johnny's eyes water. He spits again. More blood. I ask him to open wide so I can examine the wound. He gapes his mouth.

"Incisors as sharp as a dog's. No wonder you punctured your tongue."

He wiggles his tongue. The gouge is on one side of the tip. I must check the wound regularly so I can mark the healing time in my ledger.

Thelma arrives with a bag of oranges and bananas. "For the love of Zig, what's going on here?" she yells, shaking her bag of fruit at us. "Where are your shirts? Why's Johnny spitting up blood?"

Esther explains about the boxing lesson as Thelma tsk-tsks. "For goodness' sake, I can't let y'all out of my sight for five minutes."

"Why are you trying to change Boo into something he's not?" Esther says to Johnny. "It won't work. We don't change here. We're stuck. Stuck for fifty years at thirteen."

Thelma disagrees. "We grow up in other ways, Esther."

"I don't feel more mature than back in Utah," Esther says. "Except then I didn't believe in dorky Jesus, but didn't have the guts to say so."

"That's maturity, honey," says Thelma. "The guts to say what you believe."

"What about you boys?" Esther says. "Feel any different than down in America?"

"I feel more social," I say, "but I fear it comes at the cost of a lower intelligence quotient."

"Well, is it better to be dumber with friends or smarter without?" Esther asks.

"And you, Johnny?" Thelma says.

Johnny shrugs. He looks into the gray sky, perhaps checking for beauty in the cirrus clouds. "We should hit the road," he says. "It's getting late." He slips his T-shirt over his head, and I do likewise. We head back to our bicycles parked near the monkey bars, us boys walking ahead and the girls tagging behind.

"Kids at school thought you were weak, Boo," Johnny tells me. "But nothing could get to you. They'd tease you, punch you, steal your lunch, call you a geek and a f*ggot."

A geek was originally a circus artist who performed morbid acts like biting heads off live chickens and swallowing frogs. I am obviously, given my vegetarian diet, no geek. As for f*ggot, I have no tendencies, homosexual or heterosexual, and since I am forever thirteen and dislike touching others, I may never develop any sexual interest—which, from what I hear about sex, is for the best.

Johnny went on: "They'd trip you to the ground, and you'd lie there looking at something nobody noticed, like an anthill spilling out of a crack in the sidewalk."

How I miss ants! What interesting creatures! Their pheromones, their metamorphosis, their caste system, their incredible strength.

"You were strong, man. Stronger than me. Stronger than any of us."

"Thanks, Johnny," I say. "I try not to let the outer world wreak havoc with my inner one."

Johnny stops me in the playing field. "Can you do me a favor, Boo?"

"A favor?"

"When we catch Gunboy, can you be strong?" He assumes his boxer pose, dukes raised.

I nod in agreement.

"Because I'm not sure *I'm* going to be."

18	39.95

Ar

Argon

THAT NIGHT, WE STAY IN THE JIM HAWKINS DORMITORY. THE
dormitories in Town always have a few empty rooms available
to accommodate visitors. We are in Ten, a zone that looks no
different from Eleven. It has the same buildings, which resem-
ble junior highs from cities and towns across America.

Our little group dropped by the infirmaries in both zones
earlier this afternoon, but their records showed no births on or
around September 7, 1979, the date of my passing.

I enjoyed visiting the infirmaries because I could chat with
the nurses on duty about healing times of broken and fractured
limbs and collarbones. At the Mary Lennox Infirmary, we were
permitted to explore the rebirthing room for a few minutes. I
was struck again by how plain—and, frankly, non-magical—a
rebirthing bed looked. Johnny and I pulled back the covers,
peeked under the mattress, and slid underneath the bed, but
we found nothing out of the ordinary.

By nine thirty, the four of us are exhausted from cycling
and walking all day, and are in Esther and Thelma's guest room
wearing our pajamas, which we have carried with us in our
knapsacks. Thelma is applying a bandage to a blister on Esther's
foot. She tells us she plans to courier a letter to the gommers
to say we will attend their meeting scheduled a few days from
now in Six. Meanwhile, I am writing about our adventures in
my ledger at the desk, and Johnny is flipping through a map of
heaven that the do-good council gave us. Because heaven has
no printing presses, all maps are hand-drawn. The maps are in a

spiral binder, each page devoted to one zone. They are approximate since heaven has no helicopters to fly over the terrarium to take the true lay of the land.

Thelma tells Johnny he would make a fine mapmaker because he likes to draw. She is always trying to find Johnny and me an occupation. As newbies, we are not required to work for our first six months in heaven, but after that, we need to settle on some part-time job. Cook, librarian, teacher, nurse, tailor, barber, launderer, courier, bike mechanic, and window washer are a few of the positions available. Townies tend to rotate in and out of different jobs.

"I wanna be a portal seeker," Johnny says. "I wanna find a tunnel back to America and go on a haunting."

According to portal seekers, a townie can return to his hometown and "haunt" his loved ones.

"Don't be gullible, Johnny," Esther says. "There's no such thing as a portal."

"You don't know that," Thelma replies. "Maybe we ain't found one yet, but they could exist."

"I hear some kids have found portals but don't want to tell the rest of us," Johnny says. "They want to keep their finds a secret so only they can go on hauntings."

Esther says one idiotic portal seeker tried throwing himself down his dorm's garbage chute. He was convinced that our trash tumbled back to America.

"Garbage chutes are too narrow to climb into," I say. "That's an old wives' tale."

Thelma corrects me: "An old *girls*' tale is what we say here."

"Last week, I saw a kid climb into a clothes dryer and inspect the lint drawer for a portal," Esther says. "I wanted to slam the door shut and turn the machine on, but I didn't because I'm a do-gooder in training."

"Yes, honey, you're pure goodness," Thelma says, patting Esther's bandaged foot.

"If I found a portal," Johnny says, "I'd visit Rover and take him on long walks. My sister must be taking care of him. She loves animals. We were supposed to open a pet shop together. We were going to call it Zoo. When I was in my coma, Brenda kept saying, 'Don't die, Johnny. We got to open Zoo.'"

If she went on a haunting, Thelma says she would visit her three siblings, Antoine, Ralph, and Shawna. "They're in their twenties and thirties now. They might have kids of their own. I could babysit them. A ghost babysitter who'd tell them ghost stories. The kids would love me."

"I'd haunt my old church," Esther says. "I'd fly over the pulpit and tell all those pious suckers that Osmond Family albums are the devil's work."

As a ghost, Johnny says, he would also haunt any members of the Manson family still not in jail. He would scare them into becoming honorable citizens—crossing guards, accountants, librarians, school nurses. Thelma and Esther nod, since news of the Manson family's grisly activities has spread to Town through the mouths of newbies.

Johnny decides to draw Thelma and Esther posed as ghosts. He drapes them in bedsheets, their faces peeking out, but because the sheets have a blue trim, the girls look less like ghosts and more like Mother Teresa. The girls sit side by side on one bed, and Johnny sits on the other, drawing them on the sketch pad he brought along in his knapsack.

While he works, Thelma sings us Cole Porter songs. When she starts in on "Miss Otis Regrets," she stops after the first verse and says she forgot the lyrics. She switches to "Too Darn Hot." Thelma is telling a white lie: she did not forget the lyrics. As you know, Father and Mother, in the second verse of

"Miss Otis Regrets," Miss Otis draws a gun and shoots her lover down. Thelma does not want Johnny to hear a macabre story about a shooting, because she is a real do-gooder and a real friend to Johnny. And to me, too, I suppose.

By the time Johnny finishes his sketch, all four of us are yawning. We go off to the bathrooms in the corridor to prepare for bed.

In the boys' room, Johnny brushes his teeth after sprinkling his toothbrush with baking soda, which is kept in a box on the edge of the sink. This is a good sign that he is perking up; he does not always clean his teeth without my urging. While he brushes, I strip down and slip into a shower stall. I always wash thoroughly before bed, especially given the cycling we did today. It is important to wash sweat and sebum from the body: even though things like cancer are absent from heaven, acne pimples, jock itch, and offensive odors are not.

When I come out of the shower, I take my towel from my knapsack and wrap it around my waist. I do not see Johnny and assume he went back to our room, but no, he is crawling on his hands and knees under the line of sinks. He is examining the piping and maybe wondering where our water supply comes from (I often wonder that myself).

"I'm checking for portals," he says, trying to pry loose tiles from the wall under the sink using the arm of a nail clipper.

"If there were a portal here, somebody would have found it by now."

"You don't believe in portals, do you?"

"Believing in portals is like believing in telekinesis. Until you bend a spoon with your mind, I can't believe."

As I put my pajamas back on, Johnny says, "You didn't say what you'd do on a haunting, Boo. Would you go see your folks?"

I rub my towel over my hair. I feel the lump at the base of my skull, which you, Mother, call my mathematics bump. You claim it helped me learn my times tables at age five.

I tell Johnny that if I went on a haunting, I would deliver to you the book I am writing about my afterlife. However, I would not hang around long, because that would be cruel, would it not? It might give you hope, Mother and Father, that I would come back to life for good. But I would only be a ghost, not a real boy. I would never grow up. I would never go to MIT as Father wished; I would never work for NASA as Mother wanted.

I explain all this to Johnny, but he does not reply. He stays underneath the sink picking at the tiles. I go back to our room, hang my clothes in the creaky wardrobe, and climb into bed. Through the wall, I hear Thelma's whoop of laughter.

I often cannot fall asleep when I am overtired, but not tonight. I nod off in the blink of an eye (eyes, actually) with the desk lamp still on. This is a minor miracle.

Another minor miracle occurs a moment later.

Johnny comes flying into our room, yelling, "Boo, Boo!" He yanks the blanket off me and pulls me out of bed by my pajama top, popping a button. "Follow me!" he cries.

"You found a portal?" I mumble.

"No, but something almost as good."

I follow him back to the bathroom. He hurries to the last sink and points into the basin.

"Look," he whispers. "A curious object."

"Zig almighty!"

Sitting beside the drain is an insect at least two inches long. It has dark amber wings folded over its body and a black splotch on its pronotum (the plate covering its head and upper thorax).

"Is it a kind of roach?" Johnny says, leaning in close to the basin.

I nod. "Zig must have a weird sense of humor. You know what this kind of cockroach is called?"

Johnny shrugs.

"Death's head." I point to its pronotum. "That black splotch is said to look like a death mask or a vampire's scowl."

Johnny's face lights up as it has never done before in the hereafter. He lays a hand, palm up, in the sink, and the death's head (*Blaberus craniifer*) marches over his fingers and sits on his lifeline.

JOHNNY NAMES THE COCKROACH ROVER IN HONOR OF HIS BELOVED basset hound. How did Rover the roach end up in heaven? Johnny concludes that the death's head did not *pass* in the sense of die but did pass through a portal connecting life in America with life in the afterlife. The bathroom sink may be a portal, he says, nodding confidently. I am less certain. I need more evidence before drawing such a conclusion.

We are in Thelma and Esther's room, where Johnny has placed Rover in a large margarine container he found in the dorm's kitchenette. He added an apple core, pieces of orange skins, and a potato peel as food.

Thelma tells us that though a gerbil, a kitten, and a budgie have all made their way to heaven, this to her knowledge is the first insect. "Peter Peter is gonna be knocked for a loop!" she says.

Johnny puts his ear close to the margarine container. "I can hear him. It's like he's whispering something to me."

"It must be its wings rubbing together," I say, although I do not hear anything.

"Rover will bring us good luck," Johnny tells us. "He'll help us hunt down Gunboy."

Esther does not like insects. She squealed when we first showed her the death's head. "If you ask me," she says, "that gross sh*t fly of yours is a jinx."

Despite her warning, luck smiles on us in the first few days after the death's head joins our group. The sun shines brightly during this time. The skin of my companions turns browner, whereas mine, lacking melanin, remains ghostly pale (sunburns, by the way, do not exist in Town).

We make good progress during these days and visit four more zones (Nine, Two, Eight, and Seven). On the third day, in the rebirthing book at the Paul Atreides Infirmary in Seven, we come across the name of a newbie from Chicago who passed the day after me. Nina Mitchell. When we visit her at her dorm, she says she recalls little from the news reports other than "Some kids got killed at a school." When Johnny implores her to think harder, she makes a valid point: "I'd remember more if a double-decker bus hadn't run me over the next day."

"Don't get discouraged, son," Thelma tells Johnny when we are leaving Nina's dorm. "We're making headway." She reminds us about the gommer meeting we will attend tonight. "We should've gotten the gommers involved from the get-go," Thelma says. "If anybody can help us find a murderer, it's murder survivors."

We pedal all afternoon toward Six, but go at a leisurely pace because Esther's legs are too short to cycle fast on her bike, which Johnny calls her "pinkmobile." Johnny in fact prefers to go slowly because then he can easily check the faces of oncoming cyclists. Three times already on our road trip, he thought he spotted Gunboy, but when he raced after the big-eared boy, he discovered that the cyclist was simply a look-alike.

We arrive at the infirmary in Six, which is called the Deborah Blau Infirmary. The building has cracked white pillars out front, which, Johnny says, make sense because they look like broken femurs, and the infirmary is where a townie with a broken leg would go. But as she gets off her bicycle, Thelma contradicts Johnny: "The Deborah is different. It's not for broken bones. It's for broken souls."

"Broken souls?" I ask as I tie my ribbon to my bike.

"Mental cases," Esther says. "The Deborah is for kids with mental problems."

"An asylum?" I ask.

"Not exactly," Thelma says. "These kids don't have multiple personalities or think they're superheroes. They're just a little sad and confused. We even call them 'sadcons.'"

"*I'm* a little sad and confused," Esther says. "But do you see me checking in at this place for some R and R?"

"You're not sad and confused," Thelma says.

"Sometimes I am," Esther insists. "But I don't mope around in my jammies all day like a sadcon."

"What do you do when you're sad and confused, Esther?" I ask.

"I go on road trips with you mental cases."

Johnny is fishing his margarine tub out of his knapsack so Rover can also visit the Deborah. Without looking at us, he says, "I used to see a shrink."

After a pause during which Thelma, Esther, and I throw one another surprised glances, Thelma asks, "What kind of shrink, honey?"

Johnny scratches his double crown. "I can't remember exactly. His name was Harold. He had hairy nostrils and ears, which were really gross, but still he was a nice guy."

"What did you talk to him about?" Esther asks.

"I don't remember much. But I used to show him my artwork. He was really into it, especially the abstract stuff."

"But why did your folks send you to him?" Esther asks.

Johnny gives a jerky shrug. "I guess I was a sadcon." He heads up the lopsided steps of the infirmary, holding the margarine tub in front of him like a casserole he is bringing to a patient. He has punctured holes in the side and top of the tub so the death's head can peer out.

You never sent me to a psychologist, Mother and Father, but

I was often asked to speak to Mr. Buckley, a school counselor who was worried I did not fit in. It was on his advice that I practiced friendship speeches in front of my mirror at home ("Hello, Jermaine Tucker. Did you watch the Cubs game yesterday? Whom did they play against?"). Mr. Buckley said I was a round peg and all the holes at Helen Keller were square, and he grew exasperated when I explained how to bisect a round peg and cut a square shape from it. "Enough with the geometry!" he yelled, and I shut up because I dislike being yelled at. I am thankful you never hollered at me, Father and Mother.

When I saw Johnny around Sandpits or at school, he did not look sad and confused. To me, he looked like all the other boys at our school—confident, peppy, dreamy-eyed. Then again, I avoided looking too closely at my classmates.

We enter the Deborah and go to the reception desk. While Thelma explains our case to the clerk, I steal glances into the common room, where sadcons in their pajamas (as Esther predicted) are chatting or reading comic books. One boy is wearing a hat made out of twisted party balloons. These sadcons do not look different from the townies gathered in the ground-floor common room of the Frank and Joe, many of whom also don crazy hats they make themselves.

We head down the hallway to check the rebirthing book in the main office.

"Are only sad and confused thirteen-year-olds born at this infirmary?" I ask Thelma.

"No, any kind of person can be born here," she tells me. "Townies who check into the Deborah might have had serious mental problems back in America. Maybe even schizophrenia."

"The word 'schizophrenia' means 'split mind,'" I say.

"Some of them claim they were schizo back in America," Esther says, "but I bet they're exaggerating just to get out of working."

"Gunboy was crazy," Johnny says. "Maybe *he* checked in here."

We stop dead in our tracks. Esther says, "Good point."

Thelma gives us permission to wander the floors of the patient areas while she checks the rebirthing book. "But promise me, Johnny, that if you think you spot Gunboy, you won't lose your cool."

"I'll be as cool as a cucumber," Johnny says, smiling slyly.

I do not believe him.

"Cool as a jalapeño pepper is more like it," Esther says. To Thelma she promises, "We'll keep an eye on him."

Thelma reminds us that we must contact the local do-good council if we come across our killer. "It ain't up to you to dish out punishment."

"I'll be good," Johnny says. "Cross my heart and hope to redie."

As we walk down the halls of the Deborah, we peek into rooms where sadcons are reading in bed, staring out their window, or snoozing with earplugs stuffed in their ear canals. We wander around an inner courtyard filled with rosebushes. We walk through the cafeteria (today's special: rigatoni) and also through an arts and crafts class where a dozen people are making sock puppets. (Esther says that instead of sock puppets the sadcons just need "a good sock in the head." Sometimes I wonder how she managed to pass her do-gooder training courses.)

Along the way, Johnny pulls his dead-or-alive poster from his backpack to show around. "Seen this kid anywhere?" Nobody has. One sadcon we come across crouched in a stairwell says, "He looks like me." Nonsense. She is a redheaded girl mottled with freckles.

Johnny also approaches the do-good staff, again with no luck. Maybe only the most caring and kind do-gooders are posted at an asylum. They probably listen carefully to a sadcon's problems and lend helpful and heartening advice. I would not be able to hold down such a job because I have no wise advice to offer other than, "Sadness and confusion can be fleeting. Wait awhile and maybe they'll wane."

We trail up and down the hallways of the first two floors to no avail. After we are denied entry to the third floor (because the most serious mental cases reside there), Johnny decides to take Rover to the roof for some exercise. I follow him while Esther goes off to find Thelma.

The Deborah's rooftop affords a wide view of Six, the schools, the parks, the warehouses. We slip off our knapsacks and sit on the little concrete wall surrounding the roof edge. Johnny peels off the lid of the margarine tub (which he has taken to calling the roach's "camper"), and the death's head climbs out and scurries along the wall.

"We're getting warmer," Johnny says.

"I estimate eighty degrees," I reply, squinting at the yellow blur of the sun hidden behind a cloud. "But then again, it's always about eighty degrees in the afternoon in Town. I think I'll miss seasons. Back in Hoffman Estates, the leaves will be falling from the trees now."

"I'm not talking about seasons, Boo. I'm talking about Gunboy."

I stare at my roommate. His irises are the color of old Lincoln pennies. "How do you know we're getting close?"

"I feel it in my bones." He rubs his bony knees. "Maybe I'm some kind of divining rod that feels things others can't. Maybe I'm different from other kids."

Because he looks so serious, I ask if he had this sixth sense back in America.

"Possibly. That's maybe why I was sad and confused." After

a pause, he adds, "Do you remember everything about your old life, Boo?"

"I suppose so—unless Zig erased things I don't realize he erased," I say. "In general, I have a photographic memory. I even recall word for word the pages from our math textbook. Page seventy-two explained the Pythagorean theorem and how to find the length of the hypotenuse."

"My memory's a bit shot," Johnny says with an anxious look. "But then, I got shot in the head, so some of my brain might be missing. Some of my past as well. Like the summer before I came here. I don't remember much of that. Just snippets here and there."

We embarked on this road trip on the basis of Johnny's memory. Perhaps that was not very wise if his memory is shaky.

Rover returns from its jaunt and climbs onto Johnny's shoulder. "Polly wanna cracker?" he asks as if the roach were a parrot. Then a grin spreads across his face. "He's whispering again," Johnny says.

I stare at the roach on his shoulder to see if it is rubbing its wings or limbs together. It seems to be doing neither. "What do you mean it is talking?" I say.

"I can hear his little voice mumbling."

"It is not talking, Johnny."

"I hear something."

"You must have the ears of Rover the basset hound."

"My word, is that an *insect*?" a voice says.

Johnny and I turn our heads and see a girl in pajamas coming up behind us. She is the freckly sadcon from the stairwell, who believed herself to be Gunboy's spitting image. Johnny pulls Rover off his shoulder and cups the roach in his hands to show the girl. I explain that the insect is a species of cockroach known as a death's head.

"Death's head!" the girl says, her eyes round as she stares at Rover. "Well, that's the biggest sign Zig ever sent me."

The girl sits between us on the wall circling the roof. She has hazel irises—green, yellow, spots of brown—the deep, busy eyes that remind me of gas planets in a far-off galaxy.

"Zig sends you signs?" Johnny asks.

"He sends us *all* signs, but not everybody knows how to read them."

"What's my roach a sign of?"

The girl gives Johnny a sly half smile. "A portal," she says.

"Rover came out of a portal!" Johnny's eyes light up. "The drain of a sink that leads all the way back to America."

"A sink's no portal!" she exclaims. "Are you crazy?"

"So where's there a portal then?" Johnny asks, still cupping the death's head.

The girl ignores him. She strokes the insect with a fingertip. "You got wings," the girl says to Rover. "So you're a *real* angel, not frauds like the rest of us suckers."

"Despite its wings, the death's head cockroach cannot fly or even glide," I say, "unlike the American cockroach, *Periplaneta americana*."

The girl blinks at me. She has an orangey stain on the front of her pajama top, perhaps pasta sauce from lunch. The cuffs of her pajama bottoms are gray with dirt.

"Are you sad and confused?" I ask the girl. Johnny shakes his head to deter me.

"Huh?"

"Sad and confused."

She looks skyward. "Zig above, let me grow wings. Let me soar," she calls out, her brow knitted.

"I wonder why people suppose their gods are circling high above in the clouds," I say. "Couldn't they just as easily be hiding in the molecules of, say, a rock or a tree or even a roach?"

The girl's toenails, I notice, are painted purple with what looks to be pastel crayons. The death's head crawls out of Johnny's hands and onto her lap. "What a pretty baby," she murmurs, bowing her head to study the death-mask blotch on the roach's pronotum. A spot near her crown is almost bald. Either she has had a hack-job haircut or she has been plucking individual hairs from that spot.

The girl suddenly looks up, astonished. "Your roach here can talk," she says.

Johnny says, "You hear him too."

"I can't hear what he's saying, but he's saying something."

"Certain roach species can make a hissing noise," I say. "Perhaps that is what you are hearing."

A whistle sounds, Esther's trademark trill like the call of a red-winged blackbird. I glance down and see Esther and Thelma waiting in the parking lot beside our bicycles. Thelma waves. "Time to go, Johnny," I say, nodding toward the girls.

Johnny lifts Rover gently from the girl's thigh and drops it into its camper. He snaps the lid on.

"See you around," Johnny says to the girl.

She mumbles, "Don't count on it."

Johnny and I head toward the stairs. As we pull open the door to the exit, the sadcon girl shouts, "May Zig be with you!"

As we walk down the stairs, Johnny says, "That chick looks nothing at all like Gunboy."

When we reach the ground floor, he turns to me. "Holy sh*t!" he shouts, his face crumbling. He races back up the stairs.

Should I follow? His running shoes slap against the steps as he climbs higher. I assume he forgot something on the roof— his sketch pad, his pencils—though why so panicky?

I cut across the lobby (a stenciled poster reads, MY SADCON PROB IS NO CON JOB) and then leave the building through a side door and cross a stretch of lawn to the parking lot. Thelma and Esther are already astride their bicycles. I wave, but they do not see me. They are looking up. Thelma yelps and throws her ten-speed to the ground. She runs toward the Deborah.

I glance up just as the redhead girl plummets headfirst off the roof. She makes no sound as she falls. Her arms and legs do not flail. Her body does not right itself. She falls as if she is already dead. I gasp and flinch, expecting a horrible thud and the crack of her skull hitting the ground. But no thud comes. No crack either. Instead, her body passes through the solid earth as though she just dived into a calm lake.

Thelma reaches the spot where the girl disappeared. She drops to her knees. I sprint over. Thelma is panting and repeating shrilly, "Lordy! Lordy! Lordy!" Balled-up pajamas with an orange stain lie in a flowerbed of wilting black-eyed Susans. Thelma paws at the earth as though she might dig through the dirt and bring the girl back. Esther trots toward us in her ungainly run. I look up to see Johnny leaning over the edge of the roof. I fear that he, too, will leap. Never in my life have I screamed, but I do so now: *"No!"*

"REST IN PEACE" IS A COMMON EXPRESSION IN OUR HEAVEN FOR thirteen-year-olds. It is all-purpose: it can mean "take care" or "see you later" or "all the best." A townie has supper at the cafeteria, and before she heads off for an evening at the library, she says to her tablemates, "Rest in peace." I do not know how long this practice has been going on, but I never use the expression. After all, we are not resting here in heaven and we are not, for the most part, more peaceful than we were in America. (Note that I do not say "up in heaven" and "down in America," as many townies do. Who is to say which direction is which?)

"Rest in peace" is also an expression townies say when somebody repasses.

"Rest in peace, Willa Blake," sadcons and do-gooders from the Deborah say as they gather around the flowerbed where the girl from the roof disappeared. They have just buried her pajamas in the flowerbed and planted a colorful pinwheel on the spot. Every so often, the pinwheel twirls, and even though there is a slight breeze today, a patient pipes up to say that Willa herself is making it move.

My companions and I stand off to the side with our bicycles. Thelma wants us to stay awhile to show our respect. Johnny tells us he had a sudden hunch that Willa would harm herself. "I raced back to the roof, but I got there too late," he says.

The Deborah's manager, a short boy named Albert Schmidt whose baby-fat cheeks make him look ten years old, wants to know what Willa Blake said on the rooftop. "Not that it makes much difference," he admits. He tells us Willa had been talking about suicide for months.

"She talked about growing angel wings," I say. "And finding a portal."

The asylum manager shakes his head. "Oh dear," he says. "Willa was a portal seeker. She thought the portal back to America was suicide. Angels who kill themselves in heaven, she said, fly back to America as ghosts."

"How come you let her on the roof then?" Johnny says, irate. "Why didn't you tie that crazy chick to her bed?"

Albert says Willa in fact did not have roof privileges, but the staff cannot keep track of patients every hour of the day.

"If I was you, honey, I'd keep Willa's portal theory hush-hush," Thelma tells Albert. "If word gets out, we might have other portal seekers leaping from rooftops."

When the asylum manager leaves, Esther tells me suicide is rare in heaven. "Yeah, we have idiots, assh*les, and freaks up here, but nutcases who dive-bomb off buildings? No, they're scarcer than a tube of toothpaste."

It is hard to commit suicide in heaven. When a person falls from a rooftop, he usually does not die. Yes, he sustains major injuries—broken legs and ribs, concussions and the like—but he survives and eventually recovers in an infirmary. But sometimes all the king's horses and all the king's men (forgive me for being fanciful) cannot put a townie back together again. Poor Willa Blake probably died outright because she landed squarely on her head. Here in heaven, a dead person vanishes in the blink of an eye. *Poof!*

I wonder where the freckly girl is now. Is she finally dead for good? Or is she in another level of heaven with worse plumbing, uglier buildings, and lumpier gruel, cursing her bad luck because she is not back in America after all?

"I'm sorry, but Zig is supposed to cure severe sadcons before they get here," Thelma says, looking befuddled. I have noticed that she apologizes whenever Zig does something embarrassing or uncaring, as if she is to blame for his blunders.

"If Zig *is* a Mr. Fix-It," Johnny says, "he makes big freaking mistakes." He is looking skyward, as though Zig is hovering overhead and watching the fine mess he made.

"What if Zig cured Gunboy?" I say. "What if Gunboy is no longer psycho? Maybe he's now a normal boy who volunteers at a cafeteria, plays softball on his zone's team, and hopes one day to serve as a do-gooder."

Johnny glares at me. I stare back, and when I finally blink, he says, "You want to let him off the hook? Is that it? If you're wimping out, just go back to the Frank and Joe, okay?"

He looks at Thelma and Esther and sees in their faces that they, too, must have asked themselves the same question. They have probably even discussed it in private.

"Screw you all," Johnny spits. "I'll find Gunboy myself, and I don't care if he's now an angel giving harp lessons to do-gooders, I'll pound his head in with a brick." He is shouting now: *"You hear me?"*

Mourners around Willa Blake's gravesite throw us annoyed looks because we are being disrespectful. Two girls in plaid housecoats, who were wrapped in each other's arms, stop their weeping and stare at us, aghast.

Johnny's cheeks burn as he slips his knapsack on and mounts his bicycle. Thelma says, "Honey, let's get some advice tonight at the meeting, okay? Let's see what the gommers think we should do."

Johnny does not reply. He pedals away furiously without a glance back. He almost collides with more of the Deborah's sadcons who are coming to pay their respects.

I watch him speed down the street, pass a brick school, and converge with other cyclists out today, regular townies not on a quest to settle scores.

Thelma squeezes my arm and says, "Don't worry, Oliver. Everything will be hunky dory."

Esther mutters, "Don't bet your afterlife on it."

YOU DON'T HAVE TO FORGIVE, READS A POSTER HUNG IN THE
room where the gommers are meeting at the Ponyboy Curtis
School. The lettering is done in red glitter sprinkled over glue.
A second poster, also sparkly, is placed below the first. It reads,
BUT YOU CAN IF YOU WANT.

I half listen to Thelma explain the Gunboy story as I sit on
a shabby sofa with stuffing coming out of the arms. Beside me
sits Esther. Gathered around us are twenty-two gommers, some
of whom may have forgiven their murderers and some of whom
may have not.

Have I forgiven Gunboy? I am not sure. To me, he is as mysterious as Zig. Both are invisible to me. Zig works behind the
scenes. Gunboy also did his work behind the scenes (or at least
behind my back), so I find it hard to summon hatred or harbor
ill will toward my killer. If Gunboy had shot you, Mother and
Father, I could be merciless. I could pick up a brick, as Johnny
suggested, and strike Gunboy's head again and again till his
deranged mind spilled from his skull. But for my own passing,
hatred is harder to drum up because here I am in a new world
that is fascinating.

And, as I said earlier, what if Zig did indeed reform Gunboy?
Then my grasp on the brick would be shakier.

I wish Johnny were here to tell our story himself, but he did
not turn up at the Jack Merridew Dormitory, where we are to
pass the night in Six, even though he has our itinerary with him.
I left him a note in the room we are supposed to share in case he

shows up later. It reads, "Dear Johnny, when we find Gunboy, I promise to put up my dukes. Please come to the gommer meeting (see the map I drew on the back). Your friend, Oliver (a.k.a. Boo). P.S. I left you an orange in case you are hungry."

My roommate dislikes schools, so he probably will not come. For him, walking into all these schools in heaven is akin to a boy who died in an airplane crash boarding jumbo jets forevermore in his afterlife.

As usual, Thelma is wearing her purple armband this evening as a sign of her do-goodism. She gestures a lot as she speaks, making wavy hand movements like a Trojan cheerleader. "So Oliver and Johnny are in a darn pickle," she says. "Their killer may be in Town. If so, we townies have to decide what to do. As a gommer myself, I think we could use your advice."

The gommers, seated on sofas, armchairs, and throw cushions spread across the wood-slat floor, barely moved a muscle or batted an eye as Thelma told our story. They still seem spellbound. Some have their mouths hanging open. They remind me, in their patient excitement, of Rover the basset hound as he waited outside while his master delivered the *Tribune* at Sandpits.

A skinny girl with stringy hair speaks first. "Hunt Gunboy down," she says matter-of-factly, "and drown him in a lake."

For a moment nobody speaks. Then a boy says, "Stab him in the gut."

A slew of different ends for Gunboy is suggested, including "Toss him off a bridge," "Poison him with arsenic," and "Push him in front of a subway train."

Given the lack of lakes, bridges, arsenic, and subway trains in Town, I gather that the gommers are suggesting redeath penalties in line with their own murders. I look at Thelma seated beside me, expecting her to balk, but she does not. She just rubs her palms up and down her thighs as though wiping away sweat.

I glance at the glittery forgive/don't forgive posters. I am about to respond with irony, to say, "Hey, you can forgive if you want," but Esther speaks first.

"What if Johnny fingers the wrong kid?"

The gommer group leader, the girl who presumably was pushed in front of a subway train, asks, "Why would he blame some innocent boy?"

Esther clenches a sofa cushion in her lap, and I fear she will swat a gommer with it. "He never even *saw* his killer!" she shouts. "He sees this kid only in his frigging nightmares!"

The boy who was probably stabbed insists a gommer's nightmares are always very telling. "They're proof as far as I'm concerned," he says.

The bridge boy cries, "Hear, hear!" which is echoed by other gommers.

Esther ignores them and turns to me. "Maybe Johnny's a little crazy, Boo," she says, "and doesn't know what the hell he's doing."

The subway girl jumps in: "The murdered are always a little crazy when they first come here. You can't understand. You aren't one of us."

Esther says with an exasperated sigh, "Oh, get over it already."

Now all the gommers glare at her. Their faces look creepy and almost evil, as though they have just transformed into their own killers.

Thelma says, "Esther, don't be rude."

Esther huffs and then announces, "I'm going for a pee." She gets up from the sofa and asks me, "Don't you have to pee too?"

Thelma always encourages us to use the facilities before we hit the road, so I nod even though I have no urge to urinate.

Esther and I step around the gommers, who continue to give her defiant stares. When we are in the hallway, she tells me to follow her. She heads into the boys' room (because she is a feminist and deems separate rooms for boys and girls a form of segregation), then goes into a stall and closes the door. While she urinates, I wait at the sinks and wash my hands with a cake of glycerin soap.

"I'm serious about Johnny being a bit crazy," Esther says from the stall. "Was he always so weird?"

Weird? How strange that Esther considers *Johnny* the weird one. If eighth graders from Helen Keller were asked which boy, Johnny Henzel or Oliver Dalrymple, was weirder, I would win the vote by a landslide. Any students choosing Johnny would have to be odd themselves—for example, a girl like Jenny Vasquez, who keeps in her pocketbook a zoo of plastic farm animals, which she often converses with.

I tell Esther I do not recall too much overt weirdness from Johnny, but then again, he and I had little contact. I can confirm he was not prone to fistfights, rude behavior, or spitball shenanigans at school.

Esther comes out of the stall and washes her hands. She is just tall enough to see herself in the mirror hung over the sink.

"We'd better find Johnny soon before he wreaks havoc," she says.

"He won't wreak havoc," I assure her.

She takes a paper towel from a stack on the sink, dries her hands, and then crumples the towel and throws it at me. "How can I trust your instincts?" she says. "You're biased because he's your friend."

I pick up the balled-up towel from the floor and drop it in the wastebasket. "As a junior scientist and researcher, I promise you I always remain unbiased."

She raises her eyebrows.

"Neutral and objective."

"He's bloodthirsty, your friend."

"He's just a bit nervous."

"There's never been a murder here, Boo. If Johnny or the gommers kill Gunboy, who knows what'll happen. Who knows how Zig will react."

"You think he'll punish us?" This thought had not occurred to me.

"I'm not saying the ground will crack open and swallow us whole, but for sure there'll be a reckoning."

I wonder about this, because if Zig is also overseeing America, he does not seem to pencil in days of reckoning—despite the injustice, violence, and death penalties there.

"Boo, it's up to *us* to stop Johnny," Esther says. "If we don't, we'll have blood on our hands."

AFTER THE GOMMER MEETING ENDS, I AM SITTING ALONE ON THE
steps of the Ponyboy Curtis School when the boy who was
stabbed in the gut sits down beside me with a beat-up skateboard in his hands. "Howdy there," he says in a southern drawl.
One would think that in the melting pot of our heaven, townies
would eventually lose their accents, but no: the accent we come
here with is the accent we have for all fifty years.

The gommer introduces himself as Benny Baggarly. Though
blond, he is not pale like me. In fact, he is tanned, as if he has
imported sun from the American South.

He leans in close and says, "I tracked my killer down and
now I'm hauntin' that b*stard."

"Pardon me?"

"Hauntin' him. Ever hear of a hauntin'?"

"You mean you're a portal seeker?"

"Portal seeker? Portal finder's more like it."

He pulls a slip of paper from his pocket. "Don't show this to
nobody. This is for you and you alone." Benny glances around,
but no one is within hearing distance. The other gommers have
cycled off into the night.

Thelma and Esther are arguing on the lit basketball court
beside the school. I feel a tinge of sadness because it seems our
little group is breaking apart.

I unfold the slip of paper Benny passed me. On it is a hand-
drawn map of Six. An *X* is marked in the middle of Buttercup
Park, which lies on the zone's northern edge, where Six meets
Five.

Benny whispers, "We're meeting in that park tomorrow night at three in the morning."

"Who are *we*, Benny?"

"Haunters, my boy. Go on a haunting and you can do some sleuthing. Find out if your killer's down in America or up in heaven. Hell, you might even find out the kid's real name. 'Cause it sure ain't 'Gunboy.'"

I must look skeptical because Benny offers a further lure: "You can visit your folks too. Give your pa a hug, your ma a peck on the cheek. It'll do them a world of good."

I slip Benny's map into my pocket and thank him for the invitation. I have my doubts about the safety of this haunting business, however. I think of poor crazy Willa Blake and her eerie dive.

Benny gets up from the steps and dusts off the seat of his pants. "If you wanna know more, come tomorrow night. Don't be late. And make sure you come alone. This is an exclusive club. We don't invite any old Tom, Dick, and Harry."

As Benny skates off across the schoolyard, I think, *Any old Tom, Dick, and Johnny would be more like it.*

WHEN THE GIRLS AND I ARRIVE BACK AT THE JACK MERRIDEW DOR-
mitory that evening, I rush to my room in case Johnny has
returned. The intact orange still on the desk tells me that no,
he has not been here. Disappointed, I sit down on the chenille
bedspread as Thelma comes in. I wonder aloud whether Johnny
has headed back to the Frank and Joe.

Thelma's guess is that he is out showing his dead-or-alive
poster around to see if he can find Gunboy himself. "Wait a
day or two, honey, and he'll show up," she says, sitting on the
bed opposite.

"If Johnny finds Gunboy, will he really bash his head in with
a brick?"

"Oh, Oliver, that's just bravado talking. Johnny's scared.
He's as scared as any newbie gommer. Getting over murder ain't
something you do overnight."

Her comment is directed at me too. She believes I am not
emotional enough about my killing. I should not have gotten
over it already.

"Do you think Gunboy deserves a bashing?" I ask.

Thelma stares at the palms of her hands as though her life-
lines might reveal an answer. "Honest to Zig, I don't know,
sugar."

She stands up between the two beds as I lay my head back
on my pillow. Tonight she sings "Lullaby of Birdland." Her
voice sweeps through the room and flows out the window. I
expect other townies to come knocking on my door to hear

Thelma's beautiful voice better. When she sings about a weepy old willow that knows how to cry, she closes her eyes and then I close mine. After she finishes the song, Thelma bends over and plants a kiss on my forehead. Though I usually recoil from such a kiss, I do not this time, so perhaps I am changing. Just a little bit.

"Sleep tight and don't let the death's head bite," she jokes before shuffling off to the room she shares with Esther. I hope Johnny and Rover are looking after each other.

When Thelma is gone, I glance around. The walls look bare without the pencil sketches Johnny tapes up to make our temporary lodgings feel homier. My favorite sketch so far showed Esther zooming down the street on her pinkmobile, her hair and the handlebar streamers blowing horizontally. Johnny drew her in Wonder Woman's costume. He told me we were all superheroes tracking down our archenemy, Gunboy. When I asked which superhero I was, he said, "Brainboy."

Lately, I have not felt all that brainy. The smarts I have—about amoebae and nebulae and formulae—are useless here. What I need is the kind of intelligence that helps me understand why a boy might walk into a school and start shooting a gun, why one victim might forgive this boy, and why another never will.

At four thirty, I jerk awake, pulse racing because I hear Johnny screaming in his dreams, but when I flick on the light, all is quiet and the second bed is still empty. The screams must have been in *my* dreams. I drag the desk chair over to the window and sit watching the full moon and the hodgepodge of stars.

When I had insomnia back in America, I would read my school textbooks till it was light enough outside to go for an early-morning constitutional. I wish I were back at Helen Keller, memorizing the map of Africa, studying glacier formation, and conjugating verbs in French (*je meurs, tu meurs, il meurt, nous mourons . . .*).

When the pinprick stars fade out and the holy mackerel clouds float in, I change out of my pajamas and into my gym clothes. I pull on my white knee socks with red and blue stripes at the top (perhaps more Bicentennial leftovers) and then lace up my running shoes.

Outside, the day is still. No cyclists are around, and I wonder what it would be like to come to a heaven not just divided by age and nationality, but so segregated that I would be the only one inhabiting it. In other words, spending my afterlife truly alone. I shudder. I can make do with what heaven lacks: animals, cars, telephones, books of science, et al. But no people would be unbearable—even for a loner like me.

I recall a chat I had with Johnny during a morning jog almost a year ago. Though I am usually a light jogger, I was sprinting that day across a grassy backyard stretched between the buildings of Sandpits. At first, I did not notice Johnny and his sidekick, Rover, sitting on the grass and reading the *Tribune*. (Okay, the dog was not actually reading, but it *was* looking at the paper with interest.)

"You should join the track team, Boo," Johnny called out. "We could use you."

I slowed down and walked back, pushing my eyeglasses up my nose. I told Johnny I would not enjoy running with others. I did not want to hear their breathing and footsteps. The sound of my panting breath and my thumping feet was calming; the sound of theirs would be annoying and distracting.

Johnny said he could understand. "I like my alone time as well," he told me. "That's why I deliver the paper at five thirty in the morning."

Then he added something I did not understand. "Besides, I hate people too," he said.

I was taken aback. "Oh, but I don't *hate* people," I replied. "Sometimes they're a burden, especially when they interfere with my experiments and cut into my reading time, but I don't claim actual hatred."

"Yes, you do. It's okay to say so."

I did not wish to argue, so I said nothing. Johnny changed the topic. He asked, "Does anybody at school know you run?"

I shook my head as Rover yawned over the sports section.

"Do your folks know?"

Another shake of the head. Mother and Father, you assumed I went for long walks in the morning. I did not want you to know I *jogged* because you would fret about my fragile heart. Already you had sent my gym teacher a note requesting that he not put undue strain on me.

Johnny looked intrigued. "Not a soul knows?"

"You know," I said.

Johnny smiled and stretched out an ink-stained hand. "It's our secret, then," he said.

I shook his hand quickly, hoping the newsprint would not transfer to my skin.

Now, as I jog down the streets of Six, I keep an eye out for the troubled soul that is Johnny. Maybe he, too, is out early. Perhaps he slept poorly and is already up.

Few townies have risen, besides some early birds gathered with shopping carts at a warehouse, doors thrown open to reveal shelves packed with a jumble of supplies. Let us hope the delivery includes a valuable curious object—like a telescope.

I jog on till I reach Buttercup Park. Despite the portal it may contain, the park looks as ordinary as the rebirthing beds. It consists of a grassy field for sports, a scattering of trees, picnic tables, and a slightly rusty jungle gym. I have a soft spot for jungle gyms. They were invented by the son of a mathematician as a way to help children grasp three-dimensional space. This one is a 3-D grid five cubes long, five cubes wide, and five cubes tall.

I inspect the park but find nothing out of the ordinary, apart from a cracked blue vinyl Elvis Presley album probably used as a Frisbee. I do not know what I expected to find. What would a portal look like? The porthole door to a washing machine? A sewer grate? A manhole cover?

If I did find a portal, would I have the gumption to climb into it? I think of fearless brothers Frank and Joe Hardy, flashlights in hand, as they slink down a dark, mysterious passageway, as on the cover of *The Secret of the Lost Tunnel*. Maybe if Johnny were here, I would climb through a portal. I would get to the bottom of *The Mystery of the Lost Gunboy*.

24	52.00
Cr	
Chromium	

THE NEXT INFIRMARY THE GIRLS AND I VISIT, THE SAL PARADISE Infirmary in Five, is not a mental hospital. This comes as a relief because broken bones and concussions are easier for a researcher to study than sadness and confusion. My research assistant, Esther, and I check healing times with the do-good nurses. In one bed lies a comatose girl who fell off a roof in a skateboard accident. Unlike Willa Blake, she did not disappear in a bed of black-eyed Susans.

"Revoke everybody's rooftop privileges," says Esther. "We klutzy angels shouldn't be trusted up there."

Afterward, we go to the main office, where we find Thelma at a desk thumbing through a rebirthing book bound in red leatherette.

"Bingo," Thelma says. She has come across the name of a girl who passed in Illinois not so long after Johnny's own passing. "Is Schaumburg close to Hoffman Estates?" she asks.

"They're practically twin cities," I reply.

I glance over Thelma's shoulder at the ledger. Typed on the page are the names of newbies, along with their place of origin, date of passing, cause of passing, and zip code in Town. Thelma points to the name Sandy Goldberg. In the Cause of Passing column is written the word "peanut."

Sandy Goldberg | Schaumburg, IL | 28 Oct. 79 | peanut | GOB

"She was done in by a nut, Boo," Esther says. "You have that in common."

"Peanuts are no joking matter," I tell Esther. "If you're allergic, even a lick of peanut butter can trigger anaphylactic shock. Your throat swells shut and you suffocate." I hold my hands to my throat.

"Rest in peace, poor sweet girl," Thelma says as she jots down Sandy's particulars on a slip of paper.

"How do you know she's sweet?" Esther says. "She might be a b*tch. Maybe Sandy ate a peanut on purpose just to get attention."

Thelma huffs and says, "Why do you always think the worst of people?"

"Because people *are* the worst," Esther says.

Thelma looks up. "Zig give me strength," she says as though he is twirling overhead on a blade of the ceiling fan.

"Do you think Zig listens to you?" I ask.

"I hope so," Thelma says, closing the book. "But he probably has bigger fish to fry."

"He isn't our daddy to go running to when the going gets tough," Esther says. "He wants us to figure things out our selves." She picks up a snow globe paperweight from the desktop and shakes it. Inside are a tiny boy and girl sitting side by side in a sleigh and wearing matching earmuffs.

"We expect certain things from him," Esther goes on. "A place to live, food to eat, clothes to wear. And he expects certain things from us."

"What kind of things?" I ask.

"That we make do with what we have. That we show one another a little respect. That we don't let loose the worst in us."

While Thelma is returning the rebirthing book to a filing cabinet, Esther gives me a wink and slips the snow globe into Thelma's knapsack.

After we leave the infirmary, I suggest lunching in Buttercup Park, which is close by. We order takeout from a local cafeteria and then wander into the park. Thelma and Esther sit on either end of a seesaw. Given the difference in their weights, Thelma's end remains grounded and Esther's end stays lifted in the air. We eat peanut butter sandwiches, which we chose in honor of Sandy Goldberg.

Despite their argument the other day, Esther and Thelma seem good friends again. They are joking and laughing together, and Thelma is even touched when she discovers the snow globe. "North Carolina never got much snow, and Town never gets none, so this snow is all I'm ever gonna get." Still, she thinks we should return the stolen globe to the infirmary, but Esther insists it will never be missed.

I am unfamiliar with the art of friendship: the teasing, quarreling, and reconciling. How many days should a person remain upset, for example, when a friend utters an insensitive comment or shows disloyalty? These are figures I should jot in my ledger.

How many days will Johnny remain cross with me?

After I eat my sandwich, dried apricots, and wheat crackers, I make a display of picking up litter in the park and dropping it in a trash bin. In reality, I am looking for a portal. I even move the bin aside to see if a portal is hidden beneath. I find nothing.

The afternoon is spent on a wild-goose chase in search of Sandy Goldberg. Using her zip code, we track her down to her assigned dorm, where her roommate tells us she is taking a still-life painting class at the Charlie Gordon School, but at the school, the teacher tells us she dropped the class in favor of a badminton workshop at the Marcy Lewis Gymnasium. At the Marcy, a gym teacher tells us Sandy excels at the vertical jump smash and was sent on tour with the local badminton team. She will be back later in the week.

During all these travels, my bicycle chain falls off twice.

Now I really miss Johnny, because he is an expert with bicycles, whereas I end up with grease smeared over my hands and T-shirt.

That night in my room at the dorm, I try to do a drawing of my friend, a wanted *alive* poster, to show to the portal seekers attending tonight's haunting. I am no portraitist, so my sketches in my notebook look amateurish. They look like any brown-haired boy. They could even be Gunboy.

It is frustrating that the image I see in my head is not recreated on the page. I crumple up drawing after drawing and then go into the hallway to pitch them all down the garbage chute.

It is now a quarter after midnight. In two hours, I leave for the haunting, and I will not sleep tonight. No matter. I have done without sleep countless times in my life, and I will make do this time as well. Yet when I lie on my bed and look up at the twirling ceiling fan, I feel a kick of anxiety in my stomach. Though I do not believe that Zig is watching over me, I find myself repeating Thelma's words: "Zig give me strength."

25   54.94

Mn

Manganese

IN HEAVEN, WE NEED TO LOOK FOR MAGIC IN THE LITTLE THINGS.
Flashlights, for instance. Townies might not be awestruck when
they click on a flashlight and a light beam appears before them,
but when they unscrew the end of the magical metal tube and
discover it contains no batteries, awestruck is how they might
react.

Yes, believe it or not, our flashlights work fine without an
apparent energy source. But the light comes from somewhere,
does it not? What is the energy source? Maybe invisible particles float in the air to power our flashlights, desk lamps, and
streetlights. One day I will turn my attention to such conun-
drums.

In the meantime, I have a confession: just as Esther pinched
a snow globe, I stole the flashlight I hold in my hands. It comes
from a do-good station at the dorm. I hope you are not disappointed in me, Mother and Father, but these are desper-
ate times. I could have signed out a flashlight with help from
Thelma, but I did not want to alert her to my antics this evening. She would have disapproved. After all, non-do-gooders
are prohibited from wandering around after midnight unless
there is an emergency.

I am venturing out after curfew, when the streetlamps are
dark and Town seems ominous and sinister in the shadows of
the night. Not that the night is itself ominous and sinister. I will
not run into ghosts (or I will run *only* into ghosts, depending
on how you view us townies, ha-ha). I have never been afraid
of the dark. As you know, even as a youngster, I did not need a

night-light in my room. I never lay in bed petrified by a saber-toothed tiger ready to spring from my closet. I never woke in the night screaming my head off.

While I stroll down the streets with my flashlight, I wonder if Johnny will show up for this rendezvous of portal seekers. I have good news for him: our discovery of Sandy Goldberg from Schaumburg (whom Esther has taken to calling "the nutter"). Once we track down Sandy, she might be able to provide clues about Gunboy and his real identity.

If I spot another flashlight in the distance, I will click off my own light in case the person is a night monitor checking the passes that townies out after curfew are required to carry. I see no other flashlights around, however. Nighttime here is pitch-black, especially when thick clouds cloak the moon. It is also dead quiet (ha-ha). There are no screeching ambulances, passing trains, or beeping cars. Sadly, there are no chirping crickets either. The only sound comes from rustling leaves whenever a breeze picks up.

When I draw near Buttercup Park, I check my glow-in-the-dark Casper the Friendly Ghost wristwatch (a gift from Esther). It is ten to three. A light clicks on and off in the playground, so I turn off my flashlight and make a beeline toward the light. As I cross the soccer field, I see that the light comes from atop the cubic jungle gym. Somebody is perched up there and acting as a beacon. It appears to be a boy, though not Benny. Benny is short, and this boy seems to be tall. His arm with the flashlight is stretched overhead as though he is imitating the Statue of Liberty.

I stop a few yards away. "Hello there," I call.

"Zip it!" the boy barks.

I lower my voice. "Is Benny Baggarly around? He invited me to a haunting."

"Just get in your f*cking cage, dog."

A second figure climbs out from the jungle gym and moves toward me. As the beacon turns on, I see this second boy is Benny. "Come sit with me," he whispers, patting my shoulder. "But no talking." He holds a finger to his lips.

I follow Benny through the bars of the jungle gym, an awkward crawl in the flickering light. Once I am within the structure, I glance around. There are others here. I can hear them breathe and see them fleetingly when the beacon turns on. They sit in a cluster on the bottom bars. Everyone is too close for comfort. I want to ask the others if they have seen Johnny, but talking is forbidden. Minutes go by in silence. To kill time, I scan the park, but no other flashlights are approaching.

The boy standing over our heads—he must be the group leader, the head honcho of haunting—finally climbs down through the bars and perches in the very middle of the cube.

"Roll call," the boy announces. "Remember we use pseudonyms here. No real names." He passes around his flashlight, which slaps from hand to hand. Each haunter states his alias and then holds the flashlight beneath his chin, clicking it on for a second to show his face.

"Ace."

"Doug."

"Shelly."

"Funk."

"Jack Sprat."

"Crystal."

Benny says, "Ratface," and a few people giggle. The group leader hisses, "Silence!"

Lit from underneath, we all look ghostly, and so when it is my turn, I give my real alias: "Boo."

I hand the flashlight up to the leader. He says his pseudonym, "Czar," and then he also clicks the light on and shines it toward himself. In the split second before the light turns off, I glimpse a sour-faced boy with crooked features, big ears, and messy brown hair.

The dead-or-alive poster come to life.

Gunboy! Gunboy in the flesh! A pain pierces my chest. Gunboy so close I could reach over and touch him.

I recall my promise to Johnny to be strong, but I am as petrified as a child with a saber-toothed tiger growling in his closet.

In the pitch-blackness, I hear Benny Baggarly whisper, "May I go first, Czar?"

"I told you assh*les to shut the f*ck up. You don't speak unless spoken to. Understood?"

Nobody speaks.

"Understood?"

"Yes, Czar," half a dozen voices whisper back.

I do not answer. I am speechless. My heart is thumping its irregular beat, but at least the sharp pain is abating. In my head, I chant, *Hydrogen, helium, lithium, beryllium, boron, carbon, nitrogen, oxygen, fluorine.*

Did Gunboy recognize me when I shone the light in my face? Maybe I was not visible long enough. Or maybe he did not get a good look at me back at Helen Keller.

"Most of you know the drill," Gunboy says. His voice is raspy, as though he, like Johnny, yells in his sleep. "I'll take you onto the baseball diamond one at a time and portal you back home. While you wait your turn, I don't want to hear one peep out of you. If I do, I'm canceling this haunting, you f*ckers *capisce*?"

"Yes, Czar."

Neon, sodium, magnesium, aluminum, silicon.

There is a shuffling movement in our little circle as Gunboy pushes through the haunters and climbs through the bars of the jungle gym. Now he is standing outside, and the rest of us remain in our cage. "Jack Sprat, you're up first," he says. He turns on his flashlight and aims it at the ground as a boy near me wiggles out of the jungle gym. Gunboy and Jack Sprat head onto the baseball diamond, and I follow the light with my eyes, expecting any moment to hear Jack Sprat's bloodcurdling scream.

To Benny, I say, "What's going on? What will he do to Jack Sprat?"

Benny's hand clamps over my mouth. "Shush! Czar will have a conniption!"

I push his hand off. "I need to know. It's life or death!"

Somebody else whacks me in the head.

"Shut up, spaz," whispers the girl nicknamed Crystal.

I crawl through the bars of the jungle gym as someone pulls on the tail of my T-shirt, but I kick back and the person lets go. I must get away. I do not have Gunboy's real name, but perhaps with the little information I do have, Thelma can track the boy down. I am ready to hurry back to our dorm to wake the girls when I see a beam of light flitting across the baseball diamond. Gunboy is coming back! Damnation! For a moment I am frozen in place, but I shake off my fear and put up my dukes. If he shines his light on me and launches an attack, I will fight him off. The light beam draws ever closer. My nerves steel. My heart booms. My blood races.

Just before the light falls on me, a voice calls out, "Are portal seekers meeting here tonight? I'm a little late."

That voice is instantly familiar.

"Johnny Henzel?"

The cone of light sweeps across me. I put down my dukes.

"What the hell you doing here, Boo?"

Behind me, the portal seekers hiss, "Shush!"

I have not seen my roommate in a day and a half, but it seems longer. "Looking for you, Johnny," I reply. "I was out looking for you."

"Zip your mouths," Crystal calls out.

"What's her frigging problem?" Johnny says.

From out in the field comes a roar of frustration. Then this: "Can't you follow one simple order, you c*cksucking, motherf*cking retards?!"

In the baseball diamond, a circle of light is growing larger and more menacing. Our killer is racing toward us.

"Dang it all to hell!" says Denny Baggarly.

"I'll never get to Tampa now," Crystal whines.

Our killer screams, "Imbeciles! Morons!"

Johnny says, "What the f*ck's going on?"

"Gunboy," I sputter.

"Huh?" Johnny says, shining his light in my eyes.

Two galaxies colliding. That is what I expect as Johnny swings his cone of light from me to the boy rushing toward us across the playground.

For a moment, nobody speaks. The portal seekers must be trembling in their cage. In the dim light, Johnny appears stunned. His mouth drops open. He takes a step back.

Gunboy comes to a stop a few feet from Johnny. The boy looks feral, furious. His eyes glow red. His hair stands on end. "I'll murder you f*ckers," he snarls.

"Have mercy on me, Czar," Crystal from Tampa says. "I'm an innocent bystander."

"Did I tell you to speak?" Gunboy says. In the instant it takes for our killer to turn toward Crystal in the jungle gym, Johnny steps forward and raises his magical flashlight high. Then he smashes it against the boy's head.

A sharp, sickening *crack*.

Gunboy goes down in a heap. His own flashlight rolls across the sand and comes to a stop at my feet, partly lighting the scene of Johnny taking his revenge, screaming like a madman as he bashes his truncheon against the body of an unconscious boy.

In the darkness, the blood looks black.

26	55.85
Fe	
Iron	

WE RACE THROUGH THE NIGHT, JOHNNY AND I, THE BEAMS OF OUR flashlights crisscrossing, the panting of our breath overlapping, the thumping of our feet synchronizing.

We are speed demons, frantic, scared, and trying to outrun a terrible act I fear may cost us our afterlives.

29 63.55
Cu
Copper

CZAR'S REAL NAME IS CHARLES LINDBLOM. DOES THE NAME NOT sound innocent? Like the name of an upright bank manager or a gallant aviation hero making a transatlantic flight. When I shared this thought with Johnny, he said that to him the name Charles Lindblom sounded no more innocent than the name Charles Manson.

I am visiting Czar at the Sal Paradise Infirmary. I come in disguise, if a baseball cap can be considered a disguise. Johnny and I found it in our hideout. We have been holed up in an unused janitor's office in the basement of the Marcy Lewis Gymnasium next to the West Wall in Five. All day long, we hear the bouncing of basketballs overhead. The sound would drive us crazy, Johnny half-joked, were we not already so.

Another item found in our hideout is a Hardy Boys novel, in fact *The Flickering Torch Mystery*. I am pretending to read the book during my visit. The title is oddly fitting. After all, a kind of torch—a flashlight—led to Czar's stay at the Sal.

The patients here are all recovering in the same room, a long hall with cubicles separated by curtains that can be drawn for privacy. From what I have overheard, seven patients were injured in bicycle accidents and one patient, a cafeteria worker, suffered burns from an overturned pot of linguini.

Though I am telling you I am visiting Czar, Mother and Father, I am actually seated beside the bed of a girl named Nilaya Singh. I am pretending to be a friend. When a real friend of hers dropped by yesterday and asked who I was, I lied that I was one of Nilaya's skating pals. Nilaya is the girl who was skating on a rooftop, lost control of her board, and sailed off the roof. She is in a coma and not expected to wake for another week.

This is my third visit to Nilaya's bedside. Each time, I stay for about twenty minutes. Today I brought her a bouquet of wildflowers I picked outside our gymnasium hideout. Her face is puffy and bruised, and her dark hair is bound atop her head. Her arms are covered in scratches from the branches of the bushes she fell into. I sit watching her and jotting down her healing times on the bookmark inside my Hardy Boys mystery. I wish I were in fact her skating pal and had no ulterior motive. Instead, my ulterior motive lies in the next bed: Charles Lindblom. He is also in a coma, as Johnny was back in Illinois. "An eye for an eye," Johnny said about that.

Two security guards sit on either side of Czar's bed to protect him in case the person or persons who beat the patient to a pulp return to finish the job (say, smother him with a pillow).

The boy lying there is no longer recognizable from Johnny's dead-or-alive poster. His face is so battered he looks more dead than alive. His skull is fractured, his cheekbones are shattered, and his eyes are bandit-ringed with the infinity symbol. His swollen lips puff out grotesquely.

Do you wonder how a simple flashlight did such harm— especially one without batteries? Rocks. Johnny filled the empty body of his flashlight with rocks. He had a hunch he would need a weapon on the night of the haunting.

Johnny insists I visit the infirmary daily to check if Czar has passed. But despite his severe injuries, he will not. The boy is slowly healing. I do not tell Johnny this, however. "Odds are Gunboy will die and disappear," I lie. That is the outcome Johnny hopes for. Yet each day, the bruising fades and the swelling goes down a little more. Each day, Czar comes closer to waking up.

A nurse named Miss Heidi arrives to wash Czar and change his bandages. She tells the guards to take a break and then tugs the curtains partway around the bed, but I can still steal peeks through a gap. The nurse cleans Czar's wounds with cotton pads dunked in a basin of warm water that is slowly turning pink. She is a big girl, heavier even than Thelma. She is also a chatterbox. She must suppose that the comatose hear and understand voices around them (just as Johnny heard his sister and parents during his coma).

"I know what you were doing, Chucky boy," she says, running a washcloth over his limbs. "You were hypnotizing townies and messing with their heads. You convinced them a pitcher's mound was a portal they could travel through back to America. Well, I'd lay off those hauntings of yours. No good can come of them, as you learned the hard way."

One rumor going around is that Czar failed to hypnotize a townie, who grew enraged and clobbered him. A second rumor is that a demented killer is roaming Town. Yesterday I overheard other nurses at the infirmary mention both possibilities.

"Never pretend to be as magical as Zig," Miss Heidi advises. "His magic ain't perfect, and if you pretend you're him, you're bound to make a heap load of mistakes."

Miss Heidi balls up her washcloth and scrubs Czar's armpit. "Don't you fret," she says. "You'll be up and at 'em in no time, old boy."

Old boy? Why would she call Czar that?

As soon as Miss Heidi leaves with her basin of water, I slip between the curtains and hurry to the end of Czar's bed. Hung there is a clipboard with a sheet of paper that lists the patient's particulars. I grab the sheet and scan down it.

Holy moly! Charles Lindlom died on July 11, 1933!

30	65.38

Zn

Zinc

BEFORE HEADING BACK TO OUR HIDEOUT, I STOP BY A LOCAL school to pick up take-out supper from the cafeteria. I ask the server to fill plastic containers with sweet potato stew and a salad of corn and black beans.

"Portions for two, please," I say.

I am wearing my baseball cap as well as sunglasses. The server says, "Nice glasses, honey. The style suits you."

This is true irony. The sunglasses are pink and have rhinestones embedded in their frames. Johnny found the glasses in the janitor's office, and he insists I wear them outside our hideout so nobody recognizes me. I do not wear them at the infirmary, however, because I fear looking suspicious.

While I am preparing to leave, a do-gooder in a purple armband stands at the cafeteria podium, a bullhorn in one hand and a written announcement in the other. "Your attention, please," he calls out. "Given recent events, many of you have voiced concerns about being outside after dark."

Diners seated at the long tables in the cafeteria stop their chatting and lend the do-gooder their ears, a rare sight because diners usually pay no heed to special announcements (just like the students at Helen Keller).

"The do-good council assures you that the cowardly attack on a local townie a few days ago was not random. It targeted one specific boy. Some of you fear that a crazed murderer is on the loose. Our information tells us otherwise."

A redheaded boy waves his knife and fork and shouts, "I confess! I did it! I'm the murderer!" He pretends to knife the girl sitting beside him. Many diners erupt in laughter. As I scan the tables, though, I see a boy who is not laughing. It is Benny Baggarly. He is staring into his bowl of stew.

"So feel free to circulate after dark," the do-gooder goes on. "But remember that anyone caught out after midnight will face detention. Thank you."

I push my sunglasses up the bridge of my nose, grab some napkins, and hurry out of the cafeteria to bike back to our hideout.

I must tell Johnny about our mistake. Charles Lindblom is an old boy; he is not Gunboy.

I accept a share of the responsibility for what happened because I warned Johnny that Gunboy was approaching when Czar emerged fuming from the shadows. Had I kept quiet, Johnny might not have mistaken Czar for Gunboy. Yet Johnny is convinced that Czar *is* Gunboy. My roommate claims he is now sleeping "like a damn baby log," but he is lying: I hear him moaning in his sleep. We take turns sleeping on a lumpy old couch in the janitor's office; every other night, one of us sleeps on the floor atop throw pillows.

My own insomnia is worse than ever. Last night I even went out after curfew. A flashlight in hand, I returned to the scene of the crime. I climbed back into the jungle gym and sat in that makeshift jail for more than an hour. I had brought along a box cutter from our hideout and used it to make nicks up and down my arms and legs. While I did this, I thought about you, Mother and Father. How I missed your simple chats about banal things like the most effective blue shampoo to treat dandruff. How I wished I could portal back to America to see you, if only for a moment. Yet I knew from the beginning that Czar and the haunters were frauds. I knew they would not help me travel back to 222 Hill Drive.

I felt very alone in that jungle gym. I did not cry, but I did sigh deeply.

"DON'T CRY." THAT WAS WHAT JOHNNY WHISPERED TO ME IN seventh grade after I was singled out in the hallway and battered by the fists of Kevin Stein, Fred Winchester, and Jermaine Tucker. As I lay on the floor stinging from the attack, Johnny Henzel kneeled by my side and told me not to cry. "It only makes it worse," he said.

I repeated these lines to Johnny on our first night in the janitor's office. He was crouched naked in the large, rust-stained sink set up at the back of the room. He was crying because he had Czar's blood all over his face and hair. "Get it off me! Boo, get it off!" We did not have shampoo, only a cake of soap, so I used it to lather his hair and clean his face. I believe we were both in shock. As a result, I was able to touch another person without the repulsion I usually felt. All the while, he wept soundlessly.

As I scrubbed my nails into his scalp, he shivered even though the water was hot. I filled a pail with water and poured it over his head to rinse off the soap.

"I had no choice. I had to do it," he said. Soap had gone into his eyes, and he rubbed them fiercely. "The same as when you have to shoot a horse when it breaks a leg."

"A horse?"

"What Gunboy has is worse than a broken leg." He tapped his fingers against his temple. "He has a broken brain."

Johnny's bloody clothes lay beside the sink. I thought about scrubbing them, but instead I shoved them in a garbage bin. As for the rock-filled flashlight, I emptied it and wiped the canister with paper napkins.

A beach towel decorated with cartoon lobsters hung on a hook on the wall. I wrapped the towel around Johnny and helped him climb out of the sink. He slipped on a puddle of water and almost fell, but I caught him. I held him up, and he gave me a glance that said, *You're stronger than you look.*

But I did not feel strong. I felt as though my brain were also broken.

32   **72.63**

Ge

Germanium

THE JANITOR'S OFFICE IS FURNISHED SPARSELY, WITH THE RATTY
couch and five wobbly school chairs fitted with desktops the size
of a painter's palette. In one corner stands a stack of cardboard
boxes filled with a hodgepodge of forgotten supplies. In these
Johnny and I found the baseball cap, sunglasses, box cutter, and
Hardy Boys novel. I was in fact looking for clothing because I
no longer had a change of clothes with me and Johnny did not
have many clothes with him either. On my second night here,
after the Marcy closed, I went upstairs to the boys' locker room
and looked for clothing left behind in the lockers. The pickings
were slim for a boy as slim as I (ha-ha). I am swimming in the
cutoff shorts and shirt I found. No matter. I will make do.

Few people ever come down to the basement of the Marcy.
When they do, they usually just use the restroom at the foot of
the stairs, and they do not wander into the other rooms farther
down the hall. There is little reason to, since the rooms are
stocked with castoffs.

On the evening when Johnny first abandoned us, he discovered the janitor's office while exploring the center after it
closed. He broke into the Marcy by shimmying through an
unlocked basement window. His aim, he said, was to find a
place where nobody could attack him in his sleep. By "nobody,"
he meant Gunboy.

When I return from the cafeteria with our supper, I slip
through the same window and drop to the floor. I go down the
hall to the janitor's office, where Johnny is in the gym clothes I

found for him in the locker room. He is doing military push-ups on the concrete floor. He claps his hands between push-ups. His T-shirt is sweaty, and his onion smell stinks up the room.

I tell him his efforts are for naught. "Our bodies do not change. The muscle and fat we come here with are the muscle and fat we have forevermore."

"That's not fair," he says, winded.

"Afterlife ain't fair," I reply. This is something Esther always says.

I set out our supper on the floor, using paper towels as place mats. I even arrange a place setting for Rover because Johnny likes to drop a spoonful of food on a coaster for his pet roach to nibble on.

"His voice is growing stronger," he tells me as he feeds Rover. "I hear words every now and again. Today I heard the word 'suicide.'"

"Suicide?"

"It sounded like a girl's voice. I bet it's Willa talking about leaping off the Deborah."

I have never heard a peep from that creature.

I worry about Johnny's mental state.

He notices the scabs on my arms and legs. "Did you get in a fight with a pocketknife?"

"A box cutter," I say. "It is a scab-healing experiment."

He shakes his head; now it is he who is worried about my mental state. Then he asks for an update on Gunboy. I tell him Czar is stable and little has changed since yesterday. Johnny guesses that Gunboy will live for another month before succumbing to his injuries. "After all," he says, "I passed after five weeks in a coma."

"You two are treading the same path?"

Johnny runs a finger along the wings of his death's head as

the roach feeds. "We have lots in common, Gunboy and me," he says.

"What exactly?"

"Hot tempers. We're both angry b*stards."

I think back to Helen Keller and Sandpits. I do not remember Johnny being hot-tempered. I picture him seated peacefully in a corner of the library as he drew in his sketch pad. I recall him running serenely on the outdoor track that circled the football field. Everybody liked Johnny. From what I recall, our classmates did not seem to mock or bully him or try to pummel him to death in murderball as they did with me.

After Johnny and I finish supper, I rinse our plastic containers and utensils in the sink and wipe them dry with the lobster towel. Then I turn to Johnny, who is playing jacks on the floor with an old set he found in a box of junk.

I do not say, "I have something important to tell you" (he will realize it is important). I do not say, "You had better sit down" (he is already sitting) or "Hold on to your hat" (he has on a baseball cap). I just say, "Czar is forty-six years old."

Johnny misses the ball while trying to grab five jacks at once. He glances up. "What do you mean, forty-six?"

"He is an old boy. He came here decades ago."

He frowns and spits out, "Don't f*ck with me."

"Why would I f*ck with you? I make it a lifelong habit never to f*ck with anybody at any time."

I sit with him and his jacks. I explain about a group of visitors who came to see Czar just before I left the infirmary today. They talked about his skills as a magician and the shows he had put on. He would saw his assistant in half, free himself from tricky knots, and hypnotize audience members so they would crow like roosters and hop like bunnies. The shows these people talked about took place years before.

From my pocket, I pull out the patient information sheet I stole from the infirmary. I hand it to Johnny, and he reads aloud Czar's date of passing: "July eleventh, nineteen thirty-three." Then he glances up. "It says here he was trampled by a horse in Nevada."

He closes his eyes, puts down the clipboard, and rubs his temples as though his brain is also breaking.

I say nothing more. I wait. I think of injured horses put out of their misery with a bullet to the brain. Minutes click by. From out of the corner of my eye, I see Rover beetling across the far wall.

"Johnny," I finally say, "are you hunky-dory?"

His eyes blink open. "I know what must have happened, Boo," he says, his voice more gravelly than usual. "In September, this Czar kid traveled to Hoffman Estates on a haunting. He broke into somebody's house, stole a gun, and then went hunting for thirteen-year-olds."

Oh, Zig in heaven help us all.

"You do not really believe that, do you?" I ask.

He looks vexed. "It's totally possible!" he insists. "Maybe he even killed other kids during other hauntings. Maybe we aren't the only ones! We should contact the gommers, get them involved in an investigation. We might find other victims."

I sigh and say, "Czar is the victim, Johnny."

He holds up a hand and barks, "Don't!" Then he leaps up and throws open the door to our hideout. Usually he creeps down the hall to avoid making noise and attracting attention, but this time he runs. I go after him. He passes the restroom and takes the stairs two at a time to the lobby. When I reach it myself, he is already hurrying down a hall to the basketball court. The Marcy is still open, and townies are milling around. I head to the court, and when I arrive, Johnny is climbing an inner staircase to the indoor track built along the circumference of the space. Up on the track, he starts running, not simply jogging, but sprinting at top speed. Around and around he goes. Nobody else is up there. A few boys are practicing shots on the court. I leave him alone. I sit on a bench and wait for the speed demon to come down.

As I watch Johnny, I toy with the idea of leaving him here and biking home to Eleven. Maybe Thelma is back at the Frank and Joe; she will know what to do. I no longer care who killed me or why, and honestly I do not think I ever really did. I prefer investigating something less grisly—for instance, how flashlights work without batteries. That is the only kind of mystery I want to solve.

A half hour later, a do-gooder comes onto the basketball court with a bullhorn. "Closing in ten minutes," he calls out. "Wrap it up, folks."

The boys on the court head to the locker room to shower and change. They punch one another on the shoulder. They call one another "Scrotum." They laugh affably. They are part of a world Johnny used to live in. He needs to go back to that world. When he finally stops jogging and comes down from the suspended track, I have a suggestion. I almost plead with him: "Let's forget all about Gunboy, Johnny. Tomorrow morning, we can bike back to the Frank and Joe and start over again. We can get jobs. I can work for Curios, and you can teach life-drawing classes. Let's pretend we died of different causes. Me from a heart defect and you from—I don't know—a nut allergy."

My own suggestion surprises me: I do not often pretend. You will recall, Mother and Father, that as a young child I pretended briefly to be evolutionary biologist Richard Dawkins, but then I decided playacting was dishonest.

Johnny's face is drawn. Around his head he is wearing a

terry-cloth sweatband he must have found discarded on the track. "A nut allergy," he says, winded. He looks at me as though *I* am a nut.

I clarify: "Anaphylactic shock."

He stares at me a moment. "Oh, okay," he finally mumbles. Then he leaves the basketball court and heads to a drinking fountain in the lobby.

I am taken aback: I was ready for him to scold me for giving up. "Well, good, then," I call out. "Very good." I catch up to him. I put up my dukes and punch him lightly on the shoulder when he straightens up from the fountain.

Instead of going down to the basement, he heads out the front door of the Marcy. I follow him around the side of the building. He lies in the grass and stares at the darkening sky.

I remind Johnny of the day of his skitching accident back in Hoffman Estates, when he looked at the clouds awestruck. He scrunches his forehead. "Oh, yeah, I sort of remember that."

"You said you saw something beautiful, Johnny. What was it?"

"Beats me."

I lie beside him and look skyward. Pinpricks of stars dot the sky. Soon I must begin mapping them.

"Maybe I was talking about heaven," Johnny says. "The beauty awaiting us here."

I turn toward him in the grass. "Really?"

He turns toward me. A single tear drips from his eye and across the bridge of his nose. "No," he says. Then he barks a laugh and I emit several ha-ha's. Zig knows what we are laughing about.

AFTER THE MARCY CLOSES, WE SLIP THROUGH THE BASEMENT window and head back to the janitor's office. For our last night here, Johnny wants to play board games. "Like normal kids do," he says. The other day, he found a box filled with games like Don't Spill the Beans, Monopoly, Operation, and The Partridge Family Game. Clue is also among the stash, but we will not play it because, as you might imagine, Mother and Father, we are in no mood for Professor Plum bludgeoning Mr. Boddy in the billiard room with a candlestick.

Johnny reads the rules for Operation. Using tweezers, the players must act as surgeons and remove comical body parts— Adam's apple, funny bone, charley horse, spare ribs, broken heart—from a chap named Cavity Sam. In Sam's brain is a plastic ice-cream cone, alluding to brain freeze, the pain that people feel when they eat ice cream too fast.

"There is no such thing as brain damage in heaven, so Czar's brain is sure to heal fully," I tell Johnny. "Did you know certain townies have lost fingers and toes and their digits have completely grown back? Like the limbs of salamanders."

Johnny looks up from the instructions. "Don't you hack off one of your baby toes to see how long it takes to grow back," he warns.

I must admit the idea has crossed my mind.

"Czar will recover and we will accept our punishment," I continue. "Thelma will help us so we are treated fairly. We may have to clean toilets for months on end, but so be it." Maybe, as a result, I will learn more about the true nature of Town's plumbing system.

"We should apologize to Czar," I say. "It was a case of mistaken identity, like in the Hardy Boys novel *The Missing Chums*" (another book found in our hideout).

"Please, Boo, let's not talk about that guy tonight," Johnny mutters without looking up from the instructions. "What an idiotic game," he then says, throwing the instructions aside.

Instead of Operation, we play Monopoly. Johnny is the terrier; I am the wheelbarrow. Rover scampers across the board like a third game piece. At one point, Johnny holds up a Get Out of Jail Free card. Drawn on it is a cartoon fellow dressed in prison stripes. "I should hang on to this," Johnny says with a smirk.

He talks very little. He looks sad and confused even when he buys Boardwalk. We are both tired, too bushed to focus on buying railroads, hotels, and utilities, so we do not finish the game. We decide to go to bed.

Johnny puts Rover in its camper, but without the lid on so the roach can roam around at night if it wishes.

Before bed, I bathe in the big sink: I soap my hair and pour a pail of water over my head. I dry off on the lobster towel. It is my turn to sleep on the couch, but I offer it to Johnny, claiming I prefer the throw pillows on the floor. I fear that his nightmares may revisit him tonight. He might sleep more restfully on the couch.

After we turn off the lights, Johnny says, "Know any lullabies, Boo?"

I do not have Thelma's voice, but I take a shot at the Cole Porter standard "Friendship," a song that states that, in the closest friendships, people combine their individual qualities and strengths to form a "blendship." I recall that you sometimes sang this song as a duo, Mother and Father, to entertain patrons at Clippers. I sing a slower, more melancholy version than you did. In the dark, my voice sounds more tuneful and, dare I say, more angelic than I remember it from before my passing. Perhaps to offset a lower intelligence quotient, Zig tweaked my singing voice.

When I finish singing, Johnny says sleepily, "Blendship?"

"It's a portmanteau," I say.

"A poor man's toe?"

"No, a portmanteau. It means a word that combines two different words. In this case, the two are 'blend' and 'friendship.' In French, portmanteau actually means a coatrack, but in English, it also refers to a kind of suitcase with two—"

"Boo."

"Yes, Johnny?"

"Please shut up."

"IT'S ONLY A NIGHTMARE!" I CALL OUT IN MY SLEEP BECAUSE I
hear Johnny scream. One quick, panicked shout. I blink my
eyes open in the dark. Circles of light dart across the walls and
floor. The ceiling light turns on. My pupils constrict. My eyes
squint. There are people in the room. Half a dozen people.
In my daze, I think nonsensically that the janitors are here to
take their office back. Then they are on top of me. Three janitors. They throw off my sheet, grab my arms and legs, and roll
me on my side. Their faces look both grim and thrilled. My
face squashes against a pillow. I spot Rover scrabbling along
a baseboard. Across the room, janitors attack Johnny too. He
screams bloody murder. One janitor atop him pulls out a curious object—handcuffs. As my arms are wrenched behind my
back, I feel pressure on my wrists and hear a click. Janitors have
handcuffed me. I go limp, the same as when the boys piled atop
me on Halloween. So much for staying strong. Johnny does not
go limp. He scissors his legs up and down. With bare feet, he
kicks a janitor in the head. Another janitor smacks Johnny hard
in the face with the back of his hand. Johnny stops screaming
when a janitor snips off a length of duct tape from a roll and
sticks it over his mouth.

These janitors, I finally realize, are wearing purple armbands.

35 79.90

Br

Bromine

TONIGHT ZIG IS PLAYING JACKS WITH THOUSANDS OF TWINKLING stars across the heavens. I can even see the Milky Way, or at least the whitewash Zig uses to paint the night sky. I focus on the beauty above to distract myself from my ordeal.

I am tied with skipping ropes to an infirmary stretcher, which the do-gooders are now dragging across a grassy field in the manner of a sled. Before I was tied down, I was wrapped in a blanket, and so I feel like an American Indian baby bound in a papoose, except a baby would not have its hands cuffed and its mouth taped shut no matter how strict its parents might be. If my mouth were not taped, I would call out to the second stretcher being hauled across the field. I would tell Johnny not to panic. The do-gooders are kind and charitable, after all, so other than a little rope burn, we should come to no harm.

Two do-gooders are pulling a rope that is attached to my stretcher as a leash. They have flashlights to lead the way. A third do-gooder follows behind to ensure that I do not fall off. Again, if my mouth were not taped, I would tell these boys that this dramatic capture is pointless because Johnny and I planned to turn ourselves in at the crack of dawn.

Every previous night in the janitor's office, Johnny and I had placed desks in front of the door because there was no lock to keep intruders out. Tonight, however, we had not bothered. I imagine Johnny is cursing himself for that. I turn my head to catch sight of my roommate's stretcher and his own trio of escorts.

I see the other group's flashlights glimmering at the opposite end of the field. They seem to be going in a different direction. Zig almighty, the do-gooders are splitting Johnny and me up!

Where are they taking him? Maybe Czar has woken, and they will take Johnny to the infirmary so his victim can pick him out in a kind of police lineup. Or perhaps he is going straight to jail (Do not pass Go). But why would I not go with him? I am guilty too. I played a key role in this fiasco.

After my group leaves the field, my escorts drag my stretcher down an empty street. The night is silent except for the scraping sound of board against pavement, which reminds me of snowplows in Hoffman Estates. Since I am at curb level, the dark buildings we pass seem larger and more foreboding than usual. They loom over me as though passing judgment. If they had heads, they would shake them; if they had fingers, they would wag them.

My three escorts have not uttered a word yet, so I am surprised when one says, "Oh, bugger, we took a wrong turn. We should be on Phoebe Caulfield Road." They turn my sled around, and we head back and then up a different street.

I am thankful it is nighttime. If it were daytime and passersby were eyeing me, I would feel ashamed. So thank you, do-gooders, for your forethought.

We stop in front of what looks like a dorm. Two of the boys lift the stretcher to waist level and carry me down a cobblestone pathway past a hedge made up of skyrocket spruce. RHODA PEN-MARK DORMITORY is written on the sign above the front door. The dorm's doorgirl meets our group out front. She takes one look at me, the giant papoose, and says, "This ain't right."

A do-gooder says, "Just hold the door, Inez."

Inez holds the door as the do-gooders and I pass through. I am carried across the empty lobby and down the hall to a door

marked 106, like my old locker at Helen Keller. Inez fiddles
with a set of keys and finally inserts the right one and turns the
lock. "You had to gag him?" she says as she steps into the room
and flicks on the light. "He's a newbie. You could've taken pity."

"Shut up, Inez, or we'll gag *you*."

Dear Inez huffs and leaves the room.

The do-gooders set the stretcher on the bed. I look up at the
twirling ceiling fan. For some reason, I think of Czar hypnotizing the haunters. I picture him twirling a pinwheel in front of
their faces and saying, "You're feeling *sleeeeeepy*. Real *sleeeeeepy*."
I am not sleepy, however. I am wide-awake even though it must
be four in the morning.

The do-gooders untie the ropes. They roll me on my side
and unlock the handcuffs. My wrists are scrawny, so they do not
hurt from the cuffs, which I notice are plastic. Toy handcuffs!
Johnny will be mortified.

I sit up, and one of the do-gooders, a boy with a big nose,
says he will remove the duct tape. He has a bit of a British
accent. He tugs on the corner of the tape over my mouth. "This
might hurt a bit," he says. "I'll go slow."

He peels the tape, uprooting the tiny blond hairs growing
above my lip. I wince and say, "Where's Johnny Henzel?"

"We aren't permitted to say," the British boy replies.

"It was an unfortunate accident," I tell him. "We mistook
Charles Lindblom for somebody else—for our murderer, in
fact."

The two do-gooders exchange glances.

I try to play on their sympathy: "We are gommers, but we
haven't gotten over our murders yet."

My second captor, who has an American accent, says, "I
need to get the stretcher back." So I stand up, dressed only in
my boxer shorts, the blanket over my shoulders, and let the

boy drag the stretcher off the bed. He carries it from the room without a word.

"You'll sleep here tonight," the Brit says. "In the morning, the do-good president from your zone will come talk to you."

Reginald Washington is coming to save me.

"I'll be sitting outside your door, mate, in case you need anything. My name's Ringo."

"As in the Beatles."

"It's not my real name," the big-nosed boy says. "It's just what people call me. I'm from England, you see, but my family moved to Detroit a year before I passed."

"Are you my jailer, Ringo?"

"As a matter of fact, yes. I work at the Gene Forrester in Nine."

"Is that where Johnny is?"

"I am not at liberty to say."

"Look, you have to take me to Johnny Henzel right now. He is a very sensitive soul."

Ringo shakes his head.

"He is a little unstable," I say.

Ringo gives me a deadpan look. "Yes, so I heard." Then he leaves the room, shutting the door behind him.

I go to the window and draw back the dusty curtains. I try pushing up the sash, but it will not budge. In any case, even if I escaped from this room, where would I go? I cannot trot around in my underwear in search of Johnny in the dark.

Beside the window is a desk. I sit. I cannot sleep now. I will just wait for the sky to lighten and for Reginald to come. I try studying the stars in the sky, but my concentration is poor. I feel unstable myself. Zig in heaven, if I had a carving knife, I might amputate a baby toe.

36   83.80

Kr

Krypton

"HEY, OLIVER," A VOICE SAYS. "TIME TO WAKE UP. RISE AND SHINE.
Rise and shine."

A hand pats my head.

For a moment, I think the voice and the hand belong to
you, Mother. I can practically smell the citrusy hair tonic that
seeps into all your clothes on account of the hours you spend
at Clippers.

I am not dead, I think. *I am not dead after all.*

But when I blink open my eyes, the face I see is not pink and
skinny like Mother's. It is brown and chubby. "Thelma," I say,
lifting my head. "Oh, it's so nice to see you, even though you
don't smell of hair tonic."

She looks confused but then says, "It's nice to see you, too,
honey." She smiles to reveal the gap in her teeth.

I have a crick in my neck because I fell asleep seated at the
desk.

Thelma looks at the desk blotter. "What's that you drew?"

I look at the blotter. "A horse." Last night, to kill time, I
mapped stars and created a new constellation, not a winged
horse like Pegasus but a regular horse. Yet my horse has only
three legs because there were no bright stars to form a fourth.
For those who believe in omens, a three-legged horse is most
likely a bad sign. Luckily, I do not believe in omens.

"I brought you some fresh clothes, shoes, and even a toothbrush." Thelma points to the items she has laid on the bed.

"Where is Johnny? Where was he taken?"

Thelma looks away. "Why don't you get dressed, honey? Then we'll have ourselves a little talk. I need to tell you a few things."

There is something different about Thelma. It takes me a moment to pinpoint what. "You are not wearing your armband," I say.

She glances at her upper arm as though wondering where the heck the purple band went. Then she sits on the bed and hands me jeans with faint grass stains on the knees. "Well, Oliver, I'm not a do-gooder no more."

"Did you retire?" I ask, pulling on the pants.

"No, I was kicked out."

"You got fired?"

"They're calling it a 'leave of absence.' The council wasn't too happy about our escapades."

She means Johnny's escapades and mine. Our attack on Charles Lindblom lost her a job.

"Oh, Thelma, I am so sorry."

What a horrible mess I made! You would be ashamed of me, Father and Mother! Fractured skulls, lost jobs, sad and confused friends. Not to mention that poor Rover the roach was left behind at the Marcy. Johnny will be devastated if we lose his pet!

I accidentally put my T-shirt on inside out, a sign of how stupid I have become.

"I will accept any punishment the council sees fit," I tell Thelma, and she pats the bedsheets beside her so I will come and sit down.

Her eyes are anxious and red. "You won't be punished, honey. The council decided you did nothing wrong."

"But it was my fault, Thelma. I am what is called an *instigator*. I told Johnny that Charles Lindblom was Gunboy. He looked like the boy in the dead-or-alive poster."

Thelma moves her hand in the air as though erasing words on a chalkboard.

"Listen, Oliver. I need you to meet somebody."

She glances at the door. Then she gets up, goes to it, and edges it open. She nods to whoever is in the hallway.

The door pushes open and in come a boy and a girl. I stand up. The boy I recognize. It is Reginald Washington with his splotchy arms, face, and even kneecaps (he is wearing shorts, and one knee is pink and the other brown). He smiles and says, "Hello there, young fellow." As for the girl, I have never seen her before. She is very skinny, scrawnier than even I am. Two braids protrude straight out from either side of her head. Reginald nudges her toward me. She has an astonished look, as though she has seen a ghost.

To break the ice, I almost say, "Boo!"

She takes a few more steps forward, looking at me in an odd way, as though taking stock of each individual feature—my nose, my lips, my forehead.

"It's him," she says.

A sharp intake of breath from Thelma.

"Are you sure?" Reginald says.

The girl nods.

"On a scale of one to ten," Reginald says, "one being least certain and ten being most certain, how certain are you?"

A spectrum of certainty. How strange.

The girl says, "Nine and a half."

"May I ask what is going on?" I say.

"Honey, I'd like to introduce you to Sandy."

"Hi, Sandy. Nice to meet you. My name is Oliver."

"Yeah, so they told me," Sandy says, still staring.

Reginald gives Thelma a nod. Then he says, "Well, now, Sandy, we should get going. We have a long day ahead."

Sandy finally tears her attention away from my face, but just before leaving the room, she turns and gives me one last look. "Poor thing," she says.

I do not reply. I do not know why she pities me.

Once they leave, Thelma mops her forehead and cheeks with the palms of her hands.

It finally comes to me who the braided girl must be. How stupid I have been! "That was the girl from Schaumburg, Illinois," I say, and Thelma nods.

"She passed after Johnny and me. She knows who killed us, doesn't she? She knows who Gunboy is." I feel a shot of excitement. Not to mention a little ping of pain in my holey heart.

The whites of Thelma's eyes are pinker than I have ever seen them. Her face scrunches up.

"There ain't no Gunboy, Oliver."

"What? You mean we were not shot after all?"

"No, baby, there *was* a boy with a gun."

I am confused. "There was no Gunboy. There was a Gunboy. How can both be true? You are making no sense, Thelma."

Thelma takes me by the shoulders and looks me straight in the eye. Her voice comes in a raspy whisper: "Listen to me, Oliver. The boy who shot you was Johnny."

She is pulling my leg. I draw away, emitting a ha-ha to show that I like her joke, though I in fact find it distasteful.

Thelma Rudd is crying now, tears as big and fat as the wooden beads she wears in her hair. "There was only two boys, not three," she sobs. "The killer was a mental case, Oliver! A sadcon, just like Johnny said he used to be."

37   85.47
Rb
Rubidium

HYDROGEN, HELIUM, LITHIUM, BERYLLIUM, BORON, CARBON, nitrogen, oxygen, fluorine, neon, sodium, magnesium, aluminum, silicon, phosphorus, sulfur, chlorine, argon, potassium, calcium, scandium, titanium, vanadium, chromium, manganese, iron, cobalt, nickel, copper, zinc, gallium, germanium, arsenic, selenium, bromine, krypton, rubidium, strontium, yttrium, zirconium, niobium, molybdenum, technetium, ruthenium, rhodium, palladium, silver, cadmium, indium, tin, antimony, tellurium, iodine, xenon, cesium, barium, lanthanum, cerium, praseodymium, neodymium, promethium, samarium, europium, gadolinium, terbium, dysprosium, holmium, erbium, thulium, ytterbium, lutetium, hafnium, tantalum, tungsten, rhenium, osmium, iridium, platinum, gold, mercury, thallium, lead, bismuth, polonium, astatine, radon, francium, radium, actinium, thorium, protactinium, uranium, neptunium, plutonium, americium, curium, berkelium, californium, einsteinium, fermium, mendelevium, nobelium, lawrencium, rutherfordium, dubnium, seaborgium.

FATHER, YOU GAVE JOHNNY HIS LAST REAL HAIRCUT, HIS LAST before the head shave he must have had at the Schaumburg Medical Center during his stay there. The haircut occurred a few days before school started. As usual, Clippers was busy at that time of the year. Already Jermaine Tucker, Kevin Stein, Fred Winchester, and Henry Axworthy had come in, each asking for feathered bangs. You kept cracking the same lame joke about feathers: Were they Indians all of a sudden? Were Iron Eyes Cody and Sitting Bull all the rage among thirteen-year-old boys?

You like lame jokes, Father. Hence, the poster on the wall of a bald man with the caption HAIR TODAY, GONE TOMORROW. Or the sign that reads, NO, I DON'T PULL TEETH because in the Middle Ages barbers did minor surgery like tooth extraction. As you told everybody, the red stripe in the helix of the barber's pole originally stood for blood and the white stood for bandages.

In the summer and on weekends, I liked helping out at Clippers. I would sweep the floors, dust the bottles of shampoo and hair tonic kept in the shop window, and bring patrons glasses of lemonade, which, Mother, you claimed was homemade (though it came from frozen concentrate). You would both send me to fetch lunches at fast-food restaurants. You wanted fried chicken, pizzas, and hamburgers: meals I disapproved of because they cut lives short. I would bring myself back a salad and a baked potato and explain to you how cholesterol built up in arteries till plaque dammed up the blood flow to the heart or brain.

I was describing arteriolosclerosis on the Saturday afternoon in late August when Johnny Henzel stopped in, hair wild and down to his shoulders. I had not seen him all summer. Henry Axworthy, who lived in our building, had taken over Johnny's paper route. I would sometimes see Johnny's sister, Brenda, walking Rover the basset hound. She looked a lot like Johnny: same double crown, same dimple in one cheek. One time I had asked where her brother had gone, and Brenda had frowned. Why did so many people frown when I attempted small talk? She had replied with a terse "He's at camp" and then hurried off.

Johnny did not ask for feathered bangs. He asked for an eighth of an inch off (I figured his parents had sent him for a haircut he did not want). "An eighth of an inch?" Father said. "I never made it to high school, my boy. I can't even measure that small."

Johnny and Father came to a compromise: a half inch. Johnny did not talk during the haircut, or even look at himself in the mirror. He simply stared at his lap. He was wearing terry-cloth sweatbands around his wrists, like those worn by tennis players, and I thought he had probably been playing tennis at camp.

When I offered him some lemonade, it seemed he barely recognized me, as though I had changed over the summer instead of him.

Father, you trimmed the half inch and then whisked away the barber's apron. (I always admired how you did this with a flourish and without leaving any hair clippings on your patron's lap.)

After Johnny paid Mother his five dollars at the cash register, I went up to him and again attempted small talk: "So, Johnny, did you enjoy your experience at camp?"

"Camp?" he said.

"Yes, Brenda told me you were away at summer camp."

He looked at me with steely eyes. After a pause, he said, "Yeah, I was away at Camp Squeaky Fromme."

"Did you have a pleasant stay?"

He finally smiled, or at least the corners of his mouth lifted. "It was a laugh a minute, Boo, a f*cking laugh a minute."

Then he pushed through the front door of Clippers, and the bell jingled behind him.

Mother, you asked me what was wrong with Johnny. He seemed a little off that day, you said. I told you I did not know if anything was wrong. "He was away all summer at Camp Squeaky Fromme," I said.

Mother said, "Squeaky Fromme?"

"Strange name for a camp," I said. "It sounds like the name of a cartoon mouse."

"Oliver, Squeaky Fromme is the crazy lady out in California who tried to assassinate President Ford."

"That is illogical. Why would a camp be named after that lady?"

Mother gave me a smirk. "That boy's pulling your leg."

I thought, *Why would Johnny Henzel pull my leg?* Jermaine Tucker, Kevin Stein, Fred Winchester, and Henry Axworthy might do so. Johnny Henzel, however, would not. He was different. He saw the beauty in slate gray skies. He saw the appeal of early-morning solitude.

And, unlike my other classmates, he saw something good and worthy in me.

JOHNNY IS BEING HELD AT THE GENE FORRESTER JAIL AT THE FOOT of the East Wall in Nine. Reginald Washington and Sandy Goldberg are on their way there now with the intent of identifying Johnny. Sandy claims to have the facts from back in America, but the fact is that I distrust the facts in this land I now live in. The facts of America do not apply here. The fact is that an unplugged lamp should not turn on. The fact is that thirteen-year-olds should not stay thirteen for decades on end. The fact is that people should not vanish into thin air when they die. So I will need more proof of Johnny's guilt than so-called facts from a newly passed girl from Schaumburg.

"Listen to reason," Thelma says when I suggest the nut girl's memories might be faulty.

"But there is no rhyme or reason here," I reply. "If there were, heaven would not exist."

"Oh, Oliver, if you think hard about what she says," Thelma insists, "you'll see it all makes sense."

I always think hard. I am thinking hard, and nothing at all in this Zigforsaken place makes sense.

According to Thelma, Sandy Goldberg got her facts from kids at her own school in Schaumburg. Sandy swears that the shooting at Helen Keller involved only two boys, not three. She does not remember names, but she does remember faces, and she had seen ours in the newspaper. One kid was "a freak" and one kid was "a mental case," Sandy said. The mental case was suicidal and had spent the summer in a "psycho ward." As for the shooting, she could not remember a motive, or even any other details beyond the fact that "One kid was weird and the other was nuts."

Thelma tells me there was an all-points bulletin out on Johnny here in heaven. Benny Baggarly, friend of the comatose hypnotist, spotted Johnny and me at the gymnasium and reported us. It was Reginald Washington's idea to arrest Johnny in the middle of the night.

"Reginald wanted the two of you separated," Thelma tells me. "Being friends with Johnny, he said, would harm *your* mental health."

"That is bullsh*t!" I shout, and Thelma looks surprised because I usually do not shout and I usually do not swear.

"My mental health is hunky-dory," I lie.

"But, Oliver, your friend Johnny, he's . . ." She pauses, trying to find the right word, but there is no right word, so she simply says, "He killed you."

"The jury is still out on that."

Thelma and I are sitting on the bed in my temporary room. She is hugging a pillow tightly. The pillow is a stand-in for me.

"Reginald and the do-gooders are planning a trial."

"A trial?"

"They're all fired up because heaven never had a murderer before. They think Zig goofed. They want to fix his terrible mistake."

"Do you think Zig made a terrible mistake, Thelma?"

My face has probably gone even whiter, even more ghostly, because she looks at me with a mix of pity and concern, just as Sandy Goldberg did. Thelma passes me the pillow to hug. I hold it limply in my lap.

"Oliver, you know how Zig changes some townies? Like retarded kids come here a bit smarter, right? And blind kids can see. Well, maybe Zig made Johnny less crazy so he could live peaceful here in Town. Is that a terrible mistake? Maybe it is, maybe it ain't."

She is saying that just as Zig may have lowered my intelligence quotient a notch or two, he may have raised Johnny's level of sanity enough to let him function here.

"Maybe Zig changed Johnny's memories of the events," Thelma suggests. "Or maybe Johnny erased them when he shot himself in the head. Or maybe his sister lied to him when he was in his hospital bed." Thelma puts a hand over her heart. "Jiminy Crickets, I don't know what to believe, Oliver. But I don't believe what Reginald and some of them do-gooders do. They think Johnny's faking his amnesia and remembers what he did."

I push the pillow aside and stand. My legs feel wobbly, as though I have been bicycling all day. "I have to see Johnny," I say.

Thelma does not want me going to the Gene. "You're dead tired and in shock," she says. "Besides, Reginald and the do-gooders won't let you see Johnny. They won't even let *me*. Esther took off for the Gene, but she won't get permission either."

"I will not be deterred," I say.

She acquiesces, but only after forcing me to eat a bran muffin, a banana, and a handful of almonds. She then gives me her map of the zones, wishes me luck, and tells me to meet her back at the Frank and Joe tomorrow.

I hurry out of the Rhoda Penmark Dormitory, jump on a ten-speed, and pedal like mad, wishing I had thirty speeds so I could reach the jail before Reginald and Sandy do.

First, I make a quick detour to the Marcy to look for *Blaberus craniifer*. I spend fifteen minutes combing the janitor's office, even checking the Monopoly game box, but to no avail.

Rover has disappeared. I hope the roach was not trampled to death in the melee last night.

I rush back outside and hop on my bike. The trip ahead will be a long jaunt requiring me to wind through a labyrinth of streets and to cross four zones (Five, One, Two, Nine). I tell myself to focus on the road. I must not become careless and smash into a streetlamp or another cyclist. I do not want to end up in an infirmary with a concussion, which, according to my notes, takes from four to six days to heal.

Still, my mind does wander. I keep picturing the hallway of Helen Keller in the first seconds after the gun went off and everybody in the hall—except the boy who pulled the trigger and the boy who was struck by the bullet—turned toward the bang. What did my classmates and teachers see?

My mind's eye imagines everyone and everything frozen in the moment. Henry Axworthy bends over the drinking fountain, an arc of water suspended before him. Jermaine Tucker drops his math book, but it does not hit the floor. Patsy Hyde's lips peel back in a scream, exposing the braces she usually keeps hidden. Cynthia Orwell dribbles a basketball that hovers a foot from her hand. The art teacher, Mr. Huston, holds a still life drawing he is set to tape to the wall outside his classroom. Helen Keller, as always, sits posed with a mortarboard on her head in her portrait hung across from locker No. 106.

Their eyes are all turned in the same direction.

There seems to be a blind spot in my imagination, because though I see everything else perfectly, even my crumpled body at the foot of my locker, there is one thing my mind's eye cannot make out in the hallway: the face of the boy holding the gun.

THE GENE FORRESTER JAIL IS THE UGLIEST BUILDING IN TOWN. ITS concrete facade is covered in black soot as though a fire once engulfed the Gene, but there was no fire because fires do not break out here. We do not even have matches. In my first month in heaven, I often tried lighting a leaf on fire using a magnifying glass and a sunray, but the experiments proved fruitless. Only a thin wisp of smoke ever emerged.

The windows at the Gene are barred, so it is lucky that buildings do not catch on fire. Another unusual thing about this four-story building is its shape: a perfect cube. Most buildings I have seen are rectangular. Also, the Gene has no exterior architectural features. No awnings or cornices, for example.

I wonder who the inmates are. They must be townies who have committed offenses like serious acts of vandalism, disturbances of the peace, and violence causing injury. Such offenses are rare here, though. Perhaps Zig subdues certain townies in order to make the most wicked of dead American thirteen-year-olds a bit kinder and to avoid bloody clashes in Town.

I get off my bicycle and tie a red ribbon around the handlebars. The day is sunny and the sky the azure color that you, Father, call wild blue yonder. It is the kind of day when you, Mother, would remind me to wear a sun hat.

As I have mentioned, our skin never burns in heaven. Yet I do feel sunburned after my two-hour bicycle ride. Maybe I am suffering from heatstroke and should look for a water fountain. I stumble up the steps of the building into the Gene's lobby, where a long wooden desk is manned by identical twin boys whose name stickers read, TIM LU and TOM LU. They are both wearing T-shirts with a yin-yang decal. I surmise they died in an accident like a house fire or a car crash. Their passing at the same time is lucky in an odd way; after all, losing a twin must be like losing a part of yourself.

The Lu twins are reading twin copies of *The Swiss Family Robinson*. "Greetings. My name is Oliver Dalrymple. I am here to visit an inmate," I tell them. "A boy named Johnny Henzel."

"Did he say Johnny Henzel?" Tim says to Tom.

"Yes, oh my, he did," Tom says. "He *did* say Johnny Henzel." I nod.

"The boy who came in last night," Tim says to Tom as they both put down their books.

"The Grade F."

"We *never* have Grade F's. When was the last one, Tom?"

"Before our time, I'm sure. Decades ago."

"What does 'Grade F' mean?" I ask.

"Oliver Dalrymple doesn't know what 'Grade F' means."

"Of course he doesn't. He's an outsider. 'Grade F' is an insider term. It means Johnny Henzel did something really, really bad."

"Heinous, you might say."

"Yes, heinous or even egregious."

The twins do not look at me while they talk. They look at and speak to each other.

"I wonder what he could have done," Tom says.

"Maybe he kidnapped somebody," Tim replies. "We haven't had a kidnapper in ages, have we, Tom?"

"No, I can't recall the last one."

"But kidnappers are usually classified as Grade D."

"Maybe it was a series of kidnappings."

"Oh my, a serial kidnapper," Tim says. "How despicable."

I cut in: "Johnny Henzel is not a serial kidnapper. He hit a boy over the head with a flashlight."

"A flashlight?" Tim says to Tom. "That isn't Grade F. That is Grade B, or at most C, depending on the injuries."

"Also, it is alleged he shot somebody to death back in America."

"Murder!!!!" Tom shouts.

"Keep it down, Tom! You're not being very professional."

"Murder is definitely Grade F."

"Could I see Johnny Henzel?" I say.

"Oliver Dalrymple wants to visit a Grade F!"

"Even Grade D's can't have visitors. Even Grade D's are in solitary confinement on the fourth floor. So imagine Grade F's!"

"But I am the boy who Johnny allegedly shot."

"Oliver Dalrymple's the victim! Oh my! Oh goodness! A shooting victim!"

"Well, this is highly unusual, don't you think, Tim?"

" 'Unprecedented' is the word that leaps to mind."

Tim and Tom Lu converse back and forth like this before deciding that one of them will check with authorities to see if Johnny can receive a visit from the boy he shot.

"*Allegedly* shot," I say as Tim pushes back his chair and heads off.

While Tim is gone, I sit on a bench in a far corner and stare at the colored floor tiles, which form a kind of circular mandala like those that Buddhist monks create out of sand. Mandalas are supposed to favor peace, but my state of mind is hardly peaceful.

People who believe in a god often think, during trying periods in their lives, that their god is testing them. Is Zig conducting some kind of experiment here in Town despite his usual hands-off policy?